SUMMER HARVEST

FORMERLY *BREAKFAST AT THE DINER*

BY SCOTT FIELDS

Outer Banks Publishing Group
Outer Banks/Raleigh

SECOND EDITION
ISBN 13 - 978-0-9906790-5-9
ISBN 10 - 0-9906790-5-5
eISBN: 9781310419195

July 2017

A KILLING IN A SMALL TOWN

Harlan Steelman owned most of the town of Bear Creek and found his way in and out of every backroom, barroom, and bedroom.

When his rival from high school, John Watson, returns to Bear Creek with his wife and son to start anew, Harlan vows to ruin John's life and take Kara, his wife, away from him.

When Harlan is found murdered, John Watson is the likely suspect and is taken into custody.

What happens next is the trial of the century for the little town of Bear Creek, but it takes a horrible twist at the end.

The Mansfield Killings

It was the worse two-week killing spree in Ohio's history. On the night of July 21, 1948, Robert Daniels and John West entered John and Nolena Niebel's house and forced the family into their car and drove them to a cornfield just off Fleming Falls Road in Mansfield.

Robert Daniels then shot each of them in the head. The brutal murders caught national attention in the media, but the killing spree didn't stop there. Three more innocent people would lose their lives at the hands of Daniels and West in the coming week.

Scott Fields tirelessly researched the killings, the capture and trial of Daniels and even interviewed a surviving member of the Niebel family to weave this tragic story into a must-read novel bringing the reader back to those dark days in the summer of 1948. It has been more than sixty years since the tragedy, and, yet, the why of it all still remains unanswered.

The killing spree is not only remembered to this day, but is an important and dark part of Mansfield lore.

SUMMER HEAT

If you read *Fifty Shades of Grey*, you'll like *Summer Heat*! When she was 17, there wasn't a man alive she would let get near her, and when she was 18, there wasn't a man she would keep away.

Women universally hated her, men continued to hold doors for her long after she passed by - just to watch her walk away.

Ninety-nine-point nine percent of the men in Steam Corners wanted her, but she only wanted one man, Spencer Deacon. The one thing that Spencer didn't want was Jessie, and his firm and undeniable rejections infuriated her.

What followed was a series of sordid events involving murder, deceit, betrayal and the conviction of an innocent man.

All books are available on Amazon in print and as an ebooks as well as available from Barnes & Noble and fine bookstores everywhere.

THE KILLING ROAD

Dale Marlowe drifted from town to town, taking odd jobs when he ran out of money until he met Rachel Armstrong and fell in love for the first time in his life.

Shortly after they were married, Dale seemed to settle into a steady job and married life until his obsession raised its ugly head.

He went back to heavy drinking and soon Rachel and Dale were arguing almost non-stop.

Dale had had enough and went back to his drifting, but this time instead of taking odd jobs, he took people's lives. Little did he know that his first victim would seal his fate.

When Erv Meyers and his brother, Kramer learned about the rape and murder of their sister, they became as obsessed as the killer to find Marlowe and bring him to justice.

What ensued was a multi-state killing spree and one of the most extensive manhunts in criminal history.

The story is based on actual events.

DEDICATED TO MY WIFE, DEB, WHO HELPED
MAKE THIS BOOK COME TO LIFE

1 WILTON'S GARAGE

At one end of town, a faded, red pickup truck stopped in front of Wilton's Garage. A gray-haired man dressed in denim work shirt and blue jeans slid across the seat and climbed from the passenger side of the vehicle.

"Sam!" he shouted as he stood in the open doorway. It was dark inside the work area of the building, and he could barely see. One light bulb dimly glowed over a workbench near the back wall. There was a sea of cars in and around the building. Some were waiting to be repaired, and others abandoned by their owners when they received their estimate for repair.

"Sam!" he shouted again. "Where the hell are you?"

"Hold your horses," a muffled voice came from under a 1987 Ford Escort. The man walked over to the driver's side of the car and found two legs protruding from under the car. "Can't ever get any work done with all the interruptions!" he said as he wiggled from under the car. Sam Wilton's head appeared, and he stared at his uninvited guest. "Not today, Frank. I'm really busy."

"I don't care if you're fixing the Pope's car. I need you to come and look at my truck."

The big man struggled to his feet. "I really don't think the Pope drives an Escort," he said. He grabbed a rag that was lying on the fender of the car and started wiping the grease from his hands. "Now, what do you want?" he asked as he walked over to the front of the truck.

"Get down on the ground with me," he said dropping to his knees.

"Really don't have time for this."

"Just get down here, Sam. I want to show you something under the truck."

"Oh, for Christ's sakes!" he said falling to his hands and knees. "What is it this time?"

"Do you see that ball joint, Sam?" he asked pointing with one hand. "It's gone bad, and I want you to replace it."

"How do you know that it's gone bad?"

"It's making a clunking noise when I turned to the right. That's how I know."

"That doesn't necessarily mean that your ball joint is bad."

"And, Mr. Wilton," he said getting to his feet. "That ball joint went bad because of the work you did on this truck last month."

You're getting senile, Frank!" shouted the mechanic. "I put shocks on the back of this thing. How do you figure that made your ball joint go bad?"

"I don't know! You tell me! You're the mechanic! All I know is that it was fine before you worked on her, and now she has a problem."

"Frank, this is a 1949 vehicle. The guys who built this thing are either dead or drooling on themselves in some nursing home. They stopped making parts for it years ago. It's worn out. It belongs in the junk pile."

"Don't talk like that in front of her, Sam!"

The mechanic stopped wiping his hands on the rag. He turned and stared at the truck and then back at the man standing in front of him. "I'll tell you what. I'll be done with this one in a couple of minutes, and then I'll check your ball joint. Ok?"

"I'm going down to the diner to get some breakfast," he said turning away. "I'll be back in an hour. By the way, you'll have to use the passenger side door. The other one's stuck."

"It's been stuck for over five years now. Do you want me to fix it for you?"

"Hell, no!" he shouted without turning around. "You cost too much! Besides, the other door works just fine. I got better things to spend my money on than that!"

₭ ₭ ₭

Springfield was a small farming community nestled between the fields of corn and soybeans. There were only three stoplights in town, and one of them hadn't worked in two years.

The population of Springfield had reached over a thousand people years ago but had steadily declined ever since the recession of the early 80's. Many of the surrounding cities and towns experienced hard times during that era. Factories closed, and people moved away. Jobs were hard to find.

In time, the economy improved, and things returned to normal, but not for Springfield. The damage caused by the economic recession of the 1980's left deep scars on the little town. What little money that was coming into the businesses downtown was from the farmers. There were many that said that if it hadn't been for them, the town would have surely died.

The downtown business district was only three blocks long with old and decayed buildings lining both sides of Main Street. Many of the businesses had occupied the same building since the turn-of-the-century, while others had served the needs of a variety of ambitious entrepreneurs who ultimately met with certain failure.

One of the most prominent members of the business community was a man who carried the nickname of Rackets. No one in town could remember his real name. Over twenty years ago, he had come to Springfield with an inheritance from his recently departed father and an ambition to open his own business.

He first opened a hardware store that remained open for just over two years. He was sure that he could compete with the other hardware in town. It had such a limited assortment of merchandise to offer. But nobody had explained to him about loyalty in a small town. Bailey's Hardware had been in business since 1890. To the people of Springfield, there was only one hardware store in town. Within a month after Rackets opened his business to the public, the novelty was gone, and the town's people were once again bringing their business to Bailey's.

A string of short-lived ventures soon followed. Undaunted, Rackets was determined not to give up. He was confident that there was a business that would succeed for him. Then in the early 90's, Rackets opened Bob's Diner. It was an instant success. He had finally found the right business for him to run. No one in town was quite sure who Bob of Bob's Diner was. Rackets had been known as Rackets since anyone could remember.

The important thing was that Rackets had finally succeeded. Nobody was quite sure why this business worked out when the rest had failed. Many believed it was because of his extraordinary size. Rackets weighed just over 300 pounds. It was said that he might not have known much about hardware, but he sure knew something about eating.

It was a large restaurant for such a small town. It was oblong in shape with booths lining both sides and a row of tables down the center to accommodate the farmers who met there every day. Rackets recognized a need for a place for farmers to congregate. They needed a place to talk about the weather, the price of soybeans, and generally share the same gossip day after day. Shortly after he opened the diner, Rackets installed the row of tables and soon had more business than he could handle.

Frank pulled open the heavy wooden door and eased it behind him. All the regulars were already there. The room was a din of loud chatter and conversation as small groups tried to talk over the others to be heard.

"Good morning, Frank!" came a chant almost in unison.

"Morning, Gentlemen," he responded as he walked past the long table of men. "You too, George," he added pointing at a man sitting next to an empty chair that was saved for him. He walked behind the counter near the cash register and poured himself a cup of coffee.

"Good morning, Frank," came a voice from behind him. Frank turned to see an extremely obese man coming out of the kitchen.

"Morning, Rackets," he replied as he started for his place at the table. "My, you're looking lovely this morning. There's a certain glow about you this morning."

"Eat shit, Frank," replied the big man as he eased himself into the booth next to the register.

"What are you doing after work tonight, Rackets," he said loudly as he took his place at the table. "You know, I'd love to have your next baby."

"Now, that conjures up an image that I could do without," said George Ridgeway.

"How are you doing, George?" asked Frank, stirring a spoon in his hot coffee.

"Well, I didn't wake up dead this morning, so I guess I'm all right."

"Hell, at our age, you can't ask for much more than that," said Frank. He took a sip of his coffee and made a face. "My God, that's strong coffee." A waitress hurried by the long table carrying a tray of food to a booth at the front of the restaurant. "Carol!" shouted Frank. "Who made the coffee this morning?"

"The boss did," she snapped without turning around.

"Well, that figures," said Frank turning to George. "Rackets never could make a decent cup of coffee." Frank paused as he watched Carol nearly run towards the kitchen to get more food. "What the hell is going on around here, George? Carol is about ready to drop from exhaustion, and Rackets actually made coffee. This place seems a little crazy this morning."

"Don't you notice anything different?" asked George with a strange looking grin.

Frank glanced around the room and then back at his friend. "What are you talking about?"

"Look around you," barked George, the smile leaving his face. "Don't you notice something missing?"

Once again, Carol hurried by with another tray of food. "That's it!" shouted Frank. "Millie's missing! Where the hell is Millie this morning?"

"Boy, nothing gets by you, does it Frank?"

"All right, smart ass! Where is she anyway?"

"The biggest piece of gossip in weeks, and you're the last one in town to hear it."

"Jesus, George. What happened?"

"Millie ran off with Joe Parker's son," announced George as he took a sip from his cup of coffee.

"Ran off? What do you mean by ran off?" asked Frank with a puzzled look. He couldn't imagine Millie doing something like that. In all the years he had known her, she had said nothing about being in love.

"As in eloped. As in married. As in had to."

Frank looked down at the other end of the table where a man was bent over a plate of sausage and eggs. "Way to go, Parker!" shouted Frank. "Because you don't like wearing condoms, my breakfast is going to be late coming to me." The man at the end of the table glanced at Frank with a puzzled look and returned to his breakfast.

"So, Millie's getting married. That's nice," said Frank turning to his friend. "It's just too bad that she's marrying Joe Parker's son. You know, there should be a law. Guys like him shouldn't be allowed to reproduce."

George stared at his friend with a puzzled look. "You seem a little grouchy this morning. Are you retaining water today? Been having cramps lately?"

"You're probably right, George. I have been a little irritable lately," said Frank. "It just seems like nothing ever changes. Do you know what I mean George?" His friend mumbled an acknowledgment as he stuck a forkful of fried potatoes in his mouth. "I come in here every day, listen to the same old stories from the same old guys, and go back home. It just seems like there should be more to it than that. Something is missing, George. What is it? What's missing in my life, George?"

"I'll tell you what's missing."

"What is it, George? What's missing in my life?"

"Somebody to take your order. I'm almost done with my breakfast, and nobody has even taken your order," said George thrusting an entire sausage link in his mouth.

"Don't worry about me," said Frank turning away from his friend. "My guess is that tray that Carol is carrying has my breakfast on it." The two men watched as the young woman weaved in and out of the chairs and tables. She stopped and set a plate of hot food in front of Frank.

"I don't know how you do it, Frank," muttered George.

"What do you mean, George?" asked his friend. "Carol knows I like my eggs over medium and hash browns on the crispy side."

"No, that's not what I meant. I'm talking about the fact that the last time you left a tip, Moses was a Cub Scout, and yet she brought your food quicker than she did mine. You didn't even have to place an order. She knew what to bring. How do you do it, Frank?"

"Women love me, George," said Frank with a smile. He stuck a fork into the pile of hash browns. "I just have that certain something that women can't resist."

"My God, will you knock it off? I'm having enough problems digesting this food."

"So, tell me, George," said Frank as he continued eating his food. "What's Rackets going to do about a waitress?"

"Some stranger came in yesterday looking for a job, and Rackets hired her on the spot. She starts tomorrow morning."

"Someone should have warned her," said Frank.

"Warned her about what?"

"Rackets. Can you imagine working for that guy? She must be one desperate woman."

"There you go again, my friend, with that sexist thinking of yours," said George.

"What in the hell are you talking about now?"

"You just naturally assume that since we're talking about a job that involves waiting on tables, we must be talking about a woman. It could have been a man who got the job, Frank. You're a sexist, Frank, and you need to come into the new century. You have old fashion thinking, and you need to be a little more sensitive."

Frank finished the last bite of his breakfast and set his fork on the empty plate. "Was it a woman who got the job, George?" he asked wiping his mouth with a napkin.

"Well, yes. I guess so."

"Then, blow it out your ass, George."

"See. That's what I'm talking about. You've got barbaric thinking. You're not a today-kind-of-guy."

Frank drank the last of his coffee and set the cup on the table. "What would you know about being a today-kind-of-guy, George?" he asked. "You wore a leisure suit to church last Sunday."

"Hey. I happen to like leisure suits," George replied. "Besides, polyester wears like iron."

"I have to be going," Frank announced as he got to his feet. He walked a few feet from the table and stopped. George turned to see that his friend had put on his reading glasses and was studying his bill.

"Be careful, Frank," he said. "Don't let them cheat you out of anything." He paid his bill at the cash register, and as he passed by the table of men, George shouted at him. "Don't worry about the tip, you tightwad. I'll take care of it."

"Hey, Frank," shouted one of the other men. "What is your tip for the day?"

"My tip for the day is don't pick up hitchhikers and don't let your meat loaf. See you gentlemen tomorrow." With that, he walked out the door of the restaurant and started for the other end of town.

In a few minutes, he had walked the length of Main Street and was soon standing in front of the garage where he had left his truck. He was satisfied that his truck must have been repaired since it had been moved to the other side of the garage.

"Did you replace that ball joint, Sam?" asked Frank.

The mechanic walked over to Frank wiping his hands with a rag. "There's nothing wrong with that ball joint," he announced. "In fact, I drove it twice around the block and couldn't hear a thing that sounded bad."

"Jesus Christ, Sam!" Frank shouted. "I'm so old I have a prostate as big as a basketball, and yet I heard it."

"Calm down," said Sam. "You're working yourself into a snit."

"I wouldn't be this way if you would just learn to fix cars!"

"Good God! You really do need a hobby or something."

"Hobby, my ass," he mumbled and started for the truck.

"Frank!" shouted the mechanic. "Watch this!" Sam sprinted to the driver's side of the truck, and, with a big smile on his face, opened the door. "How 'bout that? It works again."

Frank walked slowly around to that side of the vehicle studying the open door as if it were aberration. "I'm not paying you for it!" he snapped. The smile on Sam's face quickly disappeared. "I didn't ask you to fix it, so I don't have to pay!"

"This is my gift to you," said Sam. "Besides, it makes it easier on me when you bring it in to be fixed."

Frank became silent as he opened and closed the door several times to verify that the door was indeed fixed. Sam waited patiently for Frank to either apologize for his rude outbreak or thank him for the work that he did for free. "I got to be going," said Frank as he climbed into the driver's seat and closed the door behind him.

He started the engine and began to slowly pull away from the curb. "I'll be back in town tomorrow!" he shouted from the open window of his truck. "If I hear that clunking noise between now and then, I'll be back!" Sam slowly shook his head as he watched the vehicle lumber down the road.

The last two years had been a period of adjustment for Frank Watson. He had been married to the same woman for over forty years when, without any warning, she died of what the doctor called an aneurysm.

Frank was in shock. It happened so suddenly. The woman who was his friend, his lover, his partner, his mate was gone. The woman who had shared his bed for nearly half of a century was ripped from his arms. He was lost without her.

For the first four months, Frank didn't leave the house. He sat in his favorite rocking chair staring at the blank television screen. His son and daughter would stop by and check on him from time to time, but their visits became less frequent as the months passed.

The last several weeks, Frank seemed to be his old self. He had always been the irascible sort. Everyone in town had always described him as argumentative and quick-tempered, and now, two years after the death of his wife, it seemed that he was even worse.

The faded red truck pulled into the stone driveway that led to his garage. He parked the truck in front of the garage as he often did, got out of his truck, and followed the walk that led to the back door.

It wasn't a large farm, only about a hundred acres, but it had dark, rich soil suitable for growing just about any crop. The two-story, colonial farmhouse stood proudly just off the country road with a garage, two chicken houses, and several small buildings that sheltered the farm equipment. The barn he added later was built from scratch. It was an idealistic setting that reminded him of a Currier and Ives depiction of rural America.

His wife's friends had always described the house and the surrounding grounds as picturesque and pristinely neat in appearance. Throughout the years, the house proudly displayed its stark white coat of paint that seemed to glow to those who passed by the house. Despite the demanding hard work that summer brought to a farmer, Frank always had time to keep the lawn neatly cut and trimmed. But that all changed two years ago with the death of Ida. Old dried paint peeled from the side of the house. The barn and chicken coops were empty now. The only thing that remained was a faint odor from the generations of livestock that had come and gone. Weeds grew now where once there were none.

Frank opened the back door and closed it behind him. He walked slowly over to the kitchen sink and poured himself a glass of water. He emptied the glass and returned it to its place on the sink.

For a few moments, Frank stared out the window that was just over the sink. He could see the decay all around him. It seemed that the farm had died with his wife some two years ago. He didn't plan it that way. It just happened. He knew that his wife would have wanted him to go on with life without her, but for some reason, he just couldn't. He wanted to. He wanted desperately to get his life back to normal, but it all seemed so pointless now. He tried to focus on the things that had mattered to him before she died, but without Ida's gentle smiles, he had no reward for mowing the lawn. No hot blueberry muffins to look forward to after gathering the eggs. He hadn't realized that Ida was the centerpiece in his life until she was gone, but now the aching emptiness remained where she once was. Sometimes, he thought he could smell her perfume, and he half-expected her to breeze into the room in a new sundress she had made, giving him the same girlish smile that had melted his heart so many years ago.

Frank turned and walked across the kitchen floor. He entered the living room and eased himself into his favorite chair. Frank picked up his favorite pipe that was sitting upright on the table beside him. He carefully tapped it on an ashtray, freeing the ashes and unburned tobacco to fall from the charred bowl of the pipe. He unzipped a leather pouch and dipped the empty bowl of the pipe deep into soft, aromatic tobacco. With the skill of years of experience, he tapped the tobacco into the bowl with the exact amount of pressure. He struck a match and held it over the tobacco, lightly sucking through the pipe to make the flame dance on the tobacco. Soon he could hear the crackle of the tobacco as the fire spread throughout the bowl. Frank expelled a cloud of smoke and then held the pipe in midair allowing a small trickle of smoke to dance and flit as it ascended to the ceiling.

Frank's eyes wandered aimlessly around the living room and the hallway that led to other parts of the house. Nothing had changed in the last two years. Everything was left undisturbed. Frank wanted it that way. This was the way things were when she was alive, and that's the way they should stay. Her favorite chair remained just the way she had left it, her fingerprints still intact on the wooden arms of the chair. The occasional visitor who was invited into his home was sternly cautioned not to use that chair. They were told that it was broken and would collapse with the weight of even a child.

Frank gently puffed on his pipe, the bowl getting warmer in his hand. He removed the pipe from his mouth and carefully studied the aging pipe. The bowl was paper thin from the constant use and would soon need to be replaced. Frank made a mental note that the next time he went to town, he would try to remember to buy a new one.

He stuck the end of the pipe back into his mouth and breathed deeply. A cloud of smoke enveloped his head and stung his eyes as he began to search the room again.

His eyes stopped their search as they came to the door. He tried to avoid looking at it as he had tried for the last two years. Unfortunately, they would always eventually come to rest on the door.

It had been difficult for Frank to live in that house after the death of his wife. There were too many things that brought back too many memories. He had even considered selling the farm and moving away. But there were just too many things he couldn't give up. It was bad enough that he lost his wife. There was no way in the world that he would give up the things that were a piece of her. These were the things that he could touch and hold in his hands and would bring back a flood of sweet memories.

Frank had learned to adjust to living in this house with all its memories except for one part of the house. Behind that stark white door was a bedroom. It had been their bedroom for all those years. His wife had noted just before she died that they had never slept even one night away from each other in all the forty-two years of marriage, and, except for a vacation that had taken them out of town, they had spent every night together in that room.

Frank removed the pipe from his mouth and held it in midair as he rested his elbow on the arm of the chair. He stared at the door, his eyes unblinking. Nothing had changed in the house. Everything was the same as it was when she was alive. Since nothing had changed, he expected her, anytime, to come walking through that door. She had laid down for a nap and would soon be getting up. The door would open any minute now, and she would emerge. She would probably be well rested after her nap. He would wait here until she awoke so that he could see her smiling face when she walked through that door.

Frank jumped in his chair as the back door opened and closed with a loud bang. He looked up at the clock over the fireplace. It was ten o'clock in the morning. That could only mean one thing. Toad was here.

Toad was the name given to a woman who lived in the farmhouse just across the road. Her real name was Dorothy, but everyone knew her as Toad. It was said that when she first began to walk as an infant, she seemed to hop like a toad. Her older brother called her Toad because of it, and the name remained with her.

Frank's wife and Toad had been friends for all their lives. There was not a day that went by that the two women did not spend time together. For the last twenty years, Toad came over for coffee every morning of everyday at exactly ten o'clock. Even after the death of her life long companion, Toad continued to make coffee for Frank every morning at ten o'clock.

"Put your pants back on Frank," she shouted. "You've got company."

"Have you ever thought about knocking when you enter someone's home?" he asked without getting out of his chair.

Toad began to pour a pot of water into the coffeemaker. "From what I've seen over the last several years, I don't think I have to worry about catching you doing anything."

"Same to you, Toad," he shouted over his shoulder in the direction of the kitchen. "How exciting could your life be if you come over here every day to see me?"

She measured three scoops of coffee into a filter and slid it into the machine. "You know, Frank," she said. "Just once, I'd like to walk through that door and smell coffee already brewing."

"It'll never happen," said Frank. "I don't want you to get the idea that I can do without you."

Toad turned on the coffeemaker and stared at it briefly until water started trickling into the empty pot. She turned and walked into the living room. "So, did you make your morning trip to town to visit your playmates?"

"I sure did," he replied as he leaned back in his chair. "We solved quite a few world problems this morning."

"I doubt that," she said as she sat down on the flowered sofa. "Don't forget. I know all these idiot friends of yours."

Frank became silent as he tried to remember some of the topics of discussion. "Did you hear that Mindy down at the restaurant ran off with Joe Parker's son?"

"Where have you been, Frank. That's yesterday's news."

Frank paused for a moment. "Did you hear that she's pregnant?"

"Frank, don't insult me," she said. "I'm a woman. It's my job to know these things."

"Christ. How do you find out that stuff so fast?"

"Sorry," she replied. "If I was to tell you that, I'd have to kill you."

The gray-haired man became silent as he stared out the window that was beside him.

"Are you going to the nursing home today?" she asked.

Frank began to lightly tap the arm of the chair with his open hand. "Yes, I think I will. I try to get out there at least twice a week, and I didn't see him at all last week."

"How's he doing?"

"I don't know. Sometimes he seems that he's getting better, and then other times..."

"Does he recognize you?"

"Most of the time, he does. I'll walk up to him, and he'll call me by my name. Then, ten minutes later, he'll ask me if I've seen Frank."

Toad walked into the kitchen and poured two cups of coffee. She brought them back into the living room and gave one cup to Frank. "Are they taking good care of him, Frank?" she asked as she sat back down on the sofa.

"I don't know, Toad. He seems all right on Tuesdays, but they know that I come there every Tuesday. Last week, I stopped by on a Friday to drop off a new sweatshirt, and he was terrible. He hadn't been shaved in days, his hair was greasy, and his diaper needed to be changed."

"You need to complain to someone. Someone's not doing his job. You need to let someone know, so they can fix the problem."

"I just can't, Toad," he said. "I just can't."

"Why not?" she asked. "It's just not right what they're doing."

"I know it's not right, Toad, but how do I know what they will do to him after they get in trouble? I'm telling you, Toad. I know that I don't have any proof, but I swear there is abuse in that place. Too many cuts and bruises with the same old excuses."

Silence fell on the room. Toad took a sip of her coffee and sat back in the sofa. "I'm sorry, Frank," she said softly.

Frank said nothing. His eyes wandered around the room until they stopped at the door.

"Is today the day?" asked Toad.

He looked away and then stared at the floor. "No," he muttered. "Today is not the day."

"You know as well as I do that it's time you faced this thing. I'll do it with you."

"Maybe someday," he said without looking up, "but not today."

The room became silent. Neither said anything more as they finished their coffee.

"Well, I best be going," said Toad getting to her feet. "I'm right in the middle of doing my laundry, and you know how exciting that can be."

"You sure know the ins and outs of having a good time," Frank said, leaning forward in his chair.

"Try not to hurt yourself today, Frank." She started for the door but paused with one hand on the latch to give him a wry smile. "I can tell you're going to work yourself to death today."

Frank laughed. "See you tomorrow, Toad."

"See you later," she replied, and then she was gone.

It was late afternoon when Frank finally emerged from the house. He had just finished watching a series of game shows, a re-run of "Gilligan's Island", and two of his favorite soap operas.

He walked down the back walk and got into his truck. He pulled out of his driveway and onto the road that led to town.

The nursing home was on the other side of town, and within minutes, Frank was pulling into the parking lot. It was a large, old building that set off the road on the outskirts of town. There was room for over a hundred residents, and there was always a waiting list to get in.

Frank's father had been a resident here for the last five years. It was a shock to the town of Springfield when Ned Watson checked into Saint Mary's. Neither his friends nor the members of his family could accept the fact that Ned Watson was now wearing a diaper and was confined to a wheelchair.

He was a strong and virile man, who continued to farm his land well into his seventies. At the age of sixty-five, he had declared himself retired, but, to nobody's surprise, his retirement only lasted for a year. After a brief period of planting flowers near the house and watching television, Ned found himself back in the seat of his tractor. Retirement, or "loafing", as Ned referred to it, was not meant for this man who had worked all his life. He declared that he would work the fields of his farm until he dropped dead on his tractor.

Everyone was certain that he would do just that. The rigor and hard work of farming would most certainly take its toll on a man of his age. There was no doubt in anyone's mind that he was destined for a heart attack.

Ironically, it was not the stress of farming that caused his inevitable heart attack. It was a warm day in May when Ned was walking up to the back of the house when he noticed a weed in the flowerbed beside the back porch. He bent over to remove it when it hit him. It was a heart attack of such massive proportions that it stopped his heart from beating and him from breathing. He lay there for nearly ten minutes with his heart stopped.

It was strange what happened that day. Nobody ever could explain the course of events that occurred that led to the saving of Ned Watson's life.

Willard Kendall was the mailman at the time. He stopped in front of Ned's house to deliver to small stack of bills and advertisements. As he opened the front of the mailbox and reached out of the car with the mail, one of the letters slipped from his hand and fell to the ground.

It was a perfectly quiet summer day with hardly a leaf on a tree in motion. Suddenly, there was a gust of wind that picked the letter off the ground and moved it about ten feet. Willard got out of his car and walked towards the white envelope. Another gust of wind picked it up and sent it high into the air until it landed at the rear of the house. This time, Willard ran to the envelope. He started to bend over to pick up the elusive prize when he heard the soft whimpering of a dog. It seemed strange to Willard because he knew that Ned had never owned one.

He turned in the direction of the sound, and there lying on the ground near the back door of the house was the body of a man that Willard knew instantly as that of Ned Watson. Leaning over his head and making an almost melodic sound was a small white dog that was more of a puppy than anything else was.

Willard ran over to the man and fell to his knees. He had known CPR since high school and had even used it once to save a drowning victim when he was a lifeguard. Less than a minute later, Ned Watson's heart began to pump lifesaving blood through the already cool and stark white body.

But the damage was done. His oxygen-starved brain had been permanently damaged. Ned Watson entered the hospital a short time after that never to return to his farm again. Within four months, he was transferred to the St. Mary's Nursing Home and has been confined there ever since.

Nobody in the family wanted it that way. Nobody wanted Ned Watson seemingly locked away in a world he didn't want to belong. However, it was obvious to everybody that this had to be. He was confined to a wheel chair and could do nothing for himself. He required professional care virtually every minute of the day, and this was the only place that could provide it.

Frank got out of his car and walked to the front door of the nursing home. Reluctantly, he opened the heavy oak door and closed it behind him. He opened another door that led to a hallway down one of the wings. As he walked down the hall to his father's room, he passed by the many open doorways to the semi-private rooms. The stench of urine soaked diapers and undisposed feces seem to burn Frank's nostrils. Old men and women strapped in their wheel chairs were parked near the walls of the hallway. Many were bent over in a death-like sleep. Others babbled incessantly to no one.

Frank weaved his way through the hallway until he turned into his father's room. The old man was sitting up in his bed slightly leaning to one side. "Hi, Pop!" shouted Frank as he stopped at the side of his father's bed. "How are you doing today?"

"My ass hurts," the old man replied. "That's how it's going."

"Are those sores hurting again, Dad?"

"They never stop hurting, for Christ's sakes," he replied. "They hurt day in and day out. My ass feels like it's on fire all day long."

"Has there been a doctor in to see you lately, Dad?"

"I haven't seen a doctor in over a year!" he shouted as he began to squirm in bed.

"Dad, I know better than that," said Frank taking his father's hand. "There was a doctor in here two weeks ago. I saw him myself."

"Bullshit!" shouted the old man as he snatched his hand from his son's grip. "Damn doctors don't care about me. Hell, look at my red ass! Do you think I'd have these boils on my butt if they cared about me?"

Frank stared at his father. He pulled a chair to the side of the bed and sat down. Silence fell on the room. Frank stared at his father. Ned stared at him.

"Have you seen the President of the United States lately?" asked Frank.

"He left just before you came in."

"How old are you, Dad?"

"Twenty-two. Say, what are these dumb questions for anyhow?"

"Oh nothing, Dad," said Frank patting him on the leg. "No reason at all."

Frank leaned over and brushed a lock of hair from his father's forehead. He stared into the old man's eyes. It was hard to see him like this. A once proud and strong man, Ned Watson could seemingly do anything. No matter what it was that needed to be done, Frank could always depend on his father to be there.

He stared at his father, half smiling and dreaming of the past. "Do you remember what you used to tell me all the time, Pop?" asked Frank staring into his father's eyes. There was no reply. "You used to tell me that the world was made for the winners, and that the sick and weak were eaten by the strong. I wonder if you still believe that," he said still looking at his father. "Knowing you, Dad, as well as I do, I have no doubt that you still do."

Frank turned to look at his father's roommate who had been there for only a month. He was an old man in his nineties, whose health was failing fast. At one time, Frank tried to get to know his father's roommates. It seemed like the kind and right thing to do. But, for some reason, being Ned's roommate meant immanent and certain death. In the last five years, Ned Watson had shared his room with over twenty men, all of whom, except for his current one, were now buried in their graves. It was a standing joke in the Watson family that sharing a room with Ned Watson was the kiss of death.

"How's your roommate, Pop?" asked Frank turning to his father.

"He's fine," was his quick answer.

"And alive," added Frank.

Ned looked over at the old man, as he lay motionless in his bed. "Don't be too sure of that," he said. "Every time I look over there, I get a sudden urge to check pulses."

Frank took his father's frail hand and engulfed it into his own. He was an old man to be sure, nearly eighty-three years old. But he still had a handsome face and a full head of snow-white hair that many women of all ages still found attractive.

"Do you remember what you always used to tell me, Pop?"

"What's that, Son?"

"You always used to say that if you take care of yourself, you can get laid at any age. Do you remember that, Dad?"

"You bet I do," he replied as he squirmed to find a new position.

"So, tell me, Pop. Is it true at eighty-three? Have you gotten lucky in here?"

"No," he quickly responded.

"Oh, so your theory about women isn't true after all," said Frank. "Why is that?"

"'Cause I didn't take care of myself."

Silence fell on the room. Frank got to his feet and moved his chair back against the wall. "Well, Pop," he said. "I've got to be going, but before I do, I have to ask you the question."

"What question is that?" asked his father.

"The question that I have asked you every time that I come here. The question. The question that you should know the answer, and when you do, I'll know that your memory is back to normal."

"Well, what in the hell is the question?"

"All right, Pop. Here it goes. What did you get me for my sixteenth birthday?"

"Is that all you wanted to know?"

"Yes, that's it. What did you get me for my sixteenth birthday?"

"I don't know."

Frank patted his father on the shoulder and said, "That's all right, Dad. I'm going to keep asking that question until you, by God, remember."

"Pick another question."

"What?"

"Pick another question, Son. Who cares what you got for your birthday."

Frank leaned over and kissed his father on the forehead. "Got to go, Pop," he said. "See you later."

He started for the door when his father said, "Hey, Son."

Frank stopped and turned to the man lying in the bed. "What do you want, Pop?"

"Do us both a big favor, will you?"

"What's that, Dad?"

"That sixteenth birthday present that's been bugging you? Get over it, will you?" Frank smiled at his father's light-hearted comment. "Good bye, Dad," he said and walked out of the room.

2 THE NEW WAITRESS

The next day began with a fiery, red sun rising proudly in the eastern sky. It was after seven o'clock when Frank Watson eased himself down the steps from the back porch. He cut across the backyard towards his truck that was still parked in the driveway.

Frank climbed into the cab of the truck and turned the key. Instead of roaring to life as it had for over thirty years, there was only a faint clicking sound coming from the engine compartment. Frank tried it again. Nothing. "Damn!" he muttered as he got out of the truck and lifted the hood. He carefully examined the engine hoping to find some obvious problem that he would be able to detect. He tugged on the cables attached to the battery and checked the belts for tightness. With the hope that he had somehow, inadvertently, found the problem, he slid across the seat and turned the key. Nothing. "Damn it all!" he said much louder this time.

He got out of the truck and stormed across the yard to the barn. He swung the double doors open to reveal a freshly painted 1955 gray and red Ford tractor. He grabbed a set of jumper cables that were hanging on a hook and climbed into the cold metal seat. With the slight turn of the key, the machine instantly came to life.

He drove over to the truck and parked as close as he could to the front of the vehicle. Within seconds, he made the connections with the jumper cables and had transmitted the necessary power from the tractor to bring the tired old truck to life. He disconnected the two vehicles and climbed back into the cab.

Frank eased the truck out of his driveway and onto the road that led to town. Within minutes, he was downtown driving past the small businesses that were just waking to a new day. From the number of vehicles parked in front of the diner, Frank could see that the usual crowd was already there. He glanced at his watch and realized that he was nearly a half-hour late.

Frank pulled into the parking lot of Wilton's Garage and parked just in front of the office. He climbed out of the cab of his truck and walked over to a man whose head was buried in the engine compartment of a new pick up.

"What did I tell you," announced Frank leaning over the front of the truck.

The startled mechanic jerked his head back nearly hitting it on the open hood. He turned to his visitor who was only inches away. "Jesus, Frank!" shouted Sam. "Don't sneak up on me like that. Now, what did you say?"

"I told you so!"

"Frank, you see these cars parked all around here," he said pointing his finger. "Their owners are anxious for me to get them fixed. So, I really don't have time for your games today."

"I told you that the new ones aren't any better than my old Ford. What's the matter with that one? Need a new engine?"

"Frank, it needs an oil change. That's all. An oil change. Besides, this truck is over five years old. Of course, in your world, that is brand new, isn't it, Frank?"

"You know, Wilt. I don't have much time either. I'm already late for breakfast, so I'm going to come right to the point. You sold me a bad battery!"

Sam's mouth fell open as he stared at the man in front of him. "What did you say?"

"That battery you sold me was no good. I had to jump start her this morning."

"Frank, I don't even remember putting a battery in your truck. How long ago was it?"

"Not long ago."

"What do you mean not long ago? Was it a year, two years, three?"

"I don't know. You're the hotshot mechanic. You figure it out," said Frank walking away. "What makes the difference? The thing doesn't work, so give me a new one."

"Frank, don't get it in your head that you're getting a free battery out of this!" he shouted.

By now, Frank was nearly a block away. "I'm late for breakfast, you nitwit. Just fix my truck," he shouted without turning around.

The heavy, oak door of Bob's Cafe creaked and groaned as the man opened it and let himself in. "Good morning, Gentlemen," said Frank as he walked by the table of men.

"Good morning, Frank," came a chorus of voices.

"Little late, aren't you Frank?" asked Ben Sager. "What's wrong? Not enough sticky on your Depends this morning?"

"You know, Ben," said Frank pouring himself a cup of coffee. "The next time Leno goes on vacation, I'm sure they're going to ask you to fill in."

"Hey, Frank," shouted one of the men from the other end of the table. "Order your breakfast, and then we've got something to talk about."

Frank looked up to see who was talking as he sat down with his cup of coffee. It was Willard Miller, a farmer and former mayor of Springfield. "What's the matter with Willard?" he asked turning to George.

"I don't know," he replied. "Something's going on though. They've been talking about something important. I couldn't hear what it's all about."

"I wouldn't bet on it," said Frank taking a sip of his coffee. "Everything's a crisis with Willard. I swear he's been going through menopause for the last ten years."

"Well, there's something more interesting than Willard Miller this morning," said George with a smile. "Let me tell you."

"George, I got a pimple on my butt that's more interesting than Willard Miller."

"Wait until you see the new waitress that Rackets hired," said George grabbing Frank by the arm.

Frank looked down at his arm and then back at his friend. "Jesus, George. Control yourself. This is my last clean shirt, and you're wrinkling the hell out of it."

"She's hot," he said excitedly. "Wait 'till you see her, Frank, and the best part about her is she's divorced. You know what they say about divorced women."

"No, George. What do they say about divorced women?"

"They want it, Frank," said George. "They want it bad. They need sex. It's a proven fact."

"And where did you hear that?"

"I read it some place."

"Did you happen to read this while standing in line over at the Cash and Carry?"

"I might have. Why?"

"That explains a lot."

George grabbed his friend's arm and squeezed tightly. "Here she comes," he said excitedly.

Frank looked up to see an attractive blonde woman nearly thirty-three years old charging in their direction. Her brow was wrinkled and her lips were set in a grim line as she stopped in front of Frank.

"Well, here I am," she snapped as she put her hands on her hips."

Frank said nothing. He studied her angry face for a moment and then returned to his menu. "I'll have two eggs over easy, hash browns, and white toast. No meat today, thank you," he said folding the menu and laying it on the edge of the table. He looked up at the woman standing in front of him. Her hands were still locked in place on her hips. "Are you going to write any of this down, or are you doing some kind of Superman pose for the cover of a comic book."

"I'm here, Wise Guy," she blurted. "Give me your best shot!"

"Give you my best shot," Frank muttered with a puzzled look. "What in the hell are you talking about?"

"You're the big stud who's supposed to be able to bed me down in five minutes. I'm waiting to see your moves."

"Bed you down in five... I still don't understand what's going on here."

"One of your playmates down at the other end of the table told me that you've been bragging about how you'd have the new waitress in bed in five minutes," she said pointing at the group of men at the other end of the table. "I've been real anxious to see this man among men and the kind of moves you must have."

Frank glared at the men sitting at the other end of the table. He wasn't sure who was responsible, since they were all snickering and stealing glances. "You didn't believe those...those morons down there, did you?" The young woman said nothing. "Don't listen to anything those idiots tell you. Half of them barely made it through high school." He looked up at the woman who was staring at the men who were, by now, laughing hysterically. "Now, do you suppose I could get some breakfast?" asked Frank. The woman stood motionless for several moments and then turned and walked away.

"Way to go, Frank," muttered George as he took a sip from his coffee cup.

"What?"

"You sure know how to make a great first impression on a woman."

"Hey! Don't start with me! It's those idiots down there," said Frank pointing at the other end of the table.

"Hey, Frank," shouted Ben Sager. "Do you mind stopping by my place sometime today. I got a young heifer that needs to be bred." The entire table exploded into laughter.

"You know, Ben," said Frank with a slight grin on his face. "There's an old saying that says you shouldn't upset the one who serves you your meals. Do you know why they say that, Ben?" Silence fell on the room. The laughter turned to grins. "It's been said that there have been things added to food by upset waitresses. Did you ever hear about that, Ben?" The smile faded from Ben's face. "I don't know, but I think she seemed a little upset with you. If I were you, I'd check my food real close from now on."

"So, what did you think, Frank?" asked George. "She's a real beauty, isn't she?"

"She looks like a nice young girl trying to make a living. That's all."

"Come on. She's perfect for you."

"Perfect for me?"

"Yes, she's perfect for you. I think you should ask her out."

"Ask her out? George, I have corns on my feet that are older than her."

"So, there's a little difference in your ages."

"A little difference? Christ, I can't remember back to when I was her age."

"Here she comes with you breakfast," said George nudging his elbow into his friend's arm. "Ask her out, Frank."

The young woman stopped beside Frank and set a plate of food in front of him. "You know," said Frank looking up at the woman. "We probably got off on the wrong foot. Let's start over. My name is Frank Watson," he said extending his hand in her direction.

"You know, I really don't care what your name is, and I'd appreciate it if you and your little friends would just leave me alone. You order food, and I'll bring it to you. Is that all right with you?"

Frank said nothing. He stared intently at the woman with his hand still outstretched. She turned and stormed away. "Does this mean that we're not going out on a date?" he asked turning to George.

"I told you she wasn't for you," said George taking a sip of his coffee.

Frank stared wide-eyed at his friend, but before he could say anything, Willard Miller pulled up a chair next to him. "We have to talk," said Willard.

"Jesus, Willard, what's got you in such a tizzy?" asked Frank.

"Something's going on, Frank, and I'm not sure what it is just yet."

"Well, what's the problem?"

"You know Horace Sweeney over in Jefferson County, that high-powered real estate guy?"

"Sweeney Realtors. Yes. I know him."

"He's been sniffing around talking like he wants to buy some of the farms around here."

"Well, that's what realtors do. They get involved in the buying and selling of property."

"No, Frank. You don't understand. Horace represents some big company that wants to buy five or six farms that are next to one another. They want to buy over five hundred acres. Something just ain't right. Who would want that much farmland out here?"

"How did you find out about this?"

"Bob Howell was telling me about it. He said that they were talking to him about buying his farm only if they could get the others that are around him to sell too. It's an all or nothing kind of deal."

"Bob Howell? His place is right next to me."

"That's right. You should be hearing from them soon. See what you can find out."

"Willard?"

"Yes, Frank."

"Did anyone ever tell you how cute you look when you get excited?"

Willard sat back in his chair. "You know, Frank," he said putting his hands on his knees. "You've been nothing but a horse's ass ever since Ida died."

Silence fell on the room. Some of the men picked up their coffee cups, and others looked the other way. Frank picked up his fork and began to eat his breakfast. One of the men quietly asked one of the others what had been said, and a mumbled explanation followed.

"Sorry," muttered Willard as he got to his feet and returned to his place at the table.

"So, what do you think, Frank?" asked George to change the topic of conversation. "Are you going to ask her out?"

"George, she nearly spit on me for Christ's sakes Besides, why all this fascination with my love life? Did they cancel your favorite soap opera?"

"Because Willard was right," said George. "You are a pain in the ass."

"Thanks a lot, George. You, too?"

"I know you don't want to hear it, but you haven't been the same since Ida died. It's been two years, Frank. You need to get on with your life."

"Save your armchair psychology for someone who cares what you have to say."

"All right. I won't say anything more about it, but I knew Ida just as long as you did, and I know that she wouldn't have wanted you to become a hermit. She would have wanted you to get involved with someone. You know it as well as I do."

Frank said nothing. He stared straight ahead as he continued eating his breakfast.

"You're my best friend, Frank," said George setting his coffee cup on the table, "and I want you to be happy. I care about you and what happens to you. I know that's hard to believe, but it's true. You might be a pain in my ass, but you're still my best friend."

Frank remained silent. He finished the last bite of his breakfast and set his fork on his empty plate. He drained the last of his coffee from the cup and set it on his plate as well.

There were only a few men left at the table. Most of them had paid their bill and had already left the restaurant.

"So, what do you think, Frank?" asked George. "Now that you know how I feel about you, do you think there's a chance that we might go steady?" Frank smiled. He turned to his friend. George leaned over and stared into his eyes. "At least, consider going out on a date together. I promise to be ever so gentle."

Frank burst into laughter. "You're an asshole, George," he said grabbing his check and getting to his feet. "Has anyone ever told you that before?"

"Yeah, Frank," he said. "As a matter of fact, I think it was you who called me that at least once before."

Frank walked to the register and paid his bill. As he headed for the front door, he stopped at the long table just in front of his friend.

"No, no, no," said George waving his hands back and forth. "Frank, you keep that shiny, new nickel in your pocket. I'll get the tip today."

Frank paused for a moment as he stared at his friend. He laid a hand on his shoulder and smiled. "I must be going," he said and walked to the front of the restaurant. He opened the front door and turned to his friend. "You save yourself for me," he said and walked out the door.

Minutes later, he had walked the length of the downtown area and was standing near his truck when Sam approached him carrying a fistful of papers. He spread them out on the hood of the truck and turned to Frank.

"Did you get her fixed?" asked Frank.

"Yes, Frank," he replied. "Your beloved pickup is fixed. All it needed was a new battery."

"I told you that you sold me a bad one."

"Frank that was a five-year battery that I sold you, and it lasted fifty-two months. It wasn't exactly a bad battery."

"Well, it didn't last five years."

"I know that, Frank. I gave you nearly six dollars credit towards the new one for the eight months left on the warranty. You still owe me $39.50 for the new battery."

"My God, Sam!" shouted Frank. "You must be kidding me! Forty dollars for a battery! How do you sleep at nights, Sam?" Frank removed his wallet from his back pocket and pulled out two twenty-dollar bills. "Here, for Christ's sakes, take my money! Take all my money for crying out loud!"

Sam took the money with one hand and handed the paper work to Frank with the other. Frank studied the papers in his hand. "Where did you get these old receipts?" he asked.

"They were in the glove box of your truck," he replied. Frank took the papers and folded them up. He looked up at Sam who was still holding the money in his hand. They stared at each other for several moments.

Frank held up both hands. "Well?" he frowned.

"Well, what?"

"My change, damn it! You owe me fifty cents!"

"Jesus, Frank!" barked Sam. He dug into his pockets and pulled out a handful of coins. "All I have is pennies and nickels. I don't have any quarters."

"That's all right," he said thrusting his hand in Sam's direction. "It all spends the same." Frank thrust the assortment of coins into his pocket and climbed into his truck. He turned the key in the ignition, and the vehicle came to life. "Lucky for you!" Frank shouted to the mechanic who was still standing in the same spot.

"Always nice to see you again, Frank," he said as he watched the truck drive away.

荣 荣 荣

It was nearly eleven o'clock in the morning when the back door of Frank's farmhouse opened and closed. Toad walked across the kitchen towards the coffeepot. "Are you in the living room holding down that easy chair, Frank?" she shouted into the next room.

"So, you made it after all," Frank shouted from his chair. "I thought for a minute there that I was finally going to get some privacy. You know. Do things in my house without having to worry about some woman barging in on me."

Toad finished with the coffee maker and started for the living room. "Tell me, Frank. What would you do in your house that you would need this privacy?"

"I don't know. Maybe, I would like to walk around the house in the nude. Did you ever think about that?"

"Frank, I've seen you in the nude, and it wasn't that big of a deal," she said as she sat on the sofa.

"What are you talking about?" asked Frank turning to his guest. "When did you ever see me in the nude?"

"That time right after Ida died. Do you remember? You came walking out of the bathroom after taking a shower."

"So, what? As I recall, I had a towel at the time."

"That's right, Frank. You had a towel, but it wasn't covering anything important."

"Do you mean that you saw my privates?"

"Yes, I saw your privates, but don't worry. It wasn't that big of a deal."

"You saw me naked, and you say that it was no big deal?"

"Frank, I've seen chipmunks that were bigger than you."

"You know. It's that kind of talk will, someday, get you barred from this house."

Toad got to her feet and started for the kitchen. "Then, who would you get to fix your coffee for you and put up with your crap?"

"Good point," he shouted in the direction of the kitchen. "I guess maybe I'd better keep you. Besides, now I know why you keep coming over here."

"And why is that?" she asked as she handed a cup of coffee to her friend.

"Since you've seen me in the nude, you have this uncontrollable lust for me."

"You're right, Frank. It was too much for me," she said taking a sip from her cup. "Seeing that tiny little thing hiding in the shadow of that big stomach was a real turn-on. I'm surprised I haven't raped you by now."

Frank chuckled softly and took a sip from his hot coffee. "So, why were you so late this morning? Did you forget how to get here?"

"I was on the phone with Clara Edwards. You know what it's like to hang up on her. She was telling me about the new waitress at the restaurant. Did you happen to meet her this morning?"

"Yes. As a matter of fact, I did."

"What did you think?"

"About what?"

"About her. What did you think about her? Is she nice? Is she pretty?"

"I don't know. I really didn't pay much attention."

"Jesus, Frank. The first new woman to come to this run-down town in years and you don't remember if she was pretty or not. Well, tell me this. Do you think you might want to take her out on a date sometime?"

"Oh, for Christ's sakes. Not you too! Why does everyone think that I need a woman in my life to be happy? Besides, she's half my age. She's the same age as my kids. That almost makes it seem a little sick like I'm a pervert. The kind of guy who has Cub Scout hats under the seat of his car."

"You're worried about dating someone who's a little younger than you? My God, Frank, get with the times. You got interracial marriages, homosexuals marrying homosexuals, and, I'm sure if you looked hard enough, you could find people and farm animals tying the knot. So, don't try to shock me with a little age difference. This day and age, you have to try harder than that."

Frank gulped his coffee and then stared into the cup. He became quiet, as if he were miles away. Toad stared at her friend. She wondered if he was remembering Ida. Two years was not enough time to heal. He needed more time to get over her.

Theirs was not a common marriage. It was unique in many ways. It was holding hands after forty years of marriage. It was notes that said, "I love you" taped to the bathroom mirror and sharing a pizza and a late-night movie together. Even after all those years of marriage, they still missed one another when they were separated and felt a certain tinge of excitement when they were reunited.

Most everyone in town knew the Watsons and jealously wanted a marriage like theirs. When asked the secret of the perfect marriage, Frank Watson always replied, "There's only one ingredient for a perfect marriage, and that is we never take one another for granted."

It seemed so simple. Yet, many never really understood what it meant and those who did, found that it helped their marriage. It didn't matter to Frank and Ida. It worked for them, and that's all that mattered.

Toad drank the last of the coffee from her cup and got to her feet. "Need to be going," she announced. "I have stuff to do today."

Frank winked his eyes several times as if he were awakening from a sleep. "Well, you've already done the most important thing of the day."

"And what's that, Frank?"

"You made my coffee for me."

"Got to go, Frank. Try not to get hurt watching those soap operas. Okay?"

"Hey. The real meaning of life is right there on the television every afternoon."

Toad opened the back door and stepped outside. "Get a life, Frank," she shouted and let the door close behind her.

It was almost two o'clock in the afternoon when Frank turned off the television. He walked into the kitchen and poured himself a drink of water at the sink. After gulping down its contents, he set the empty glass on the counter and gazed out the window at the backyard.

Frank winced at what he saw. Trash littered the backyard, and the weeds grew wildly everywhere. Dried and peeling paint fell from the sides of the barn and garage leaving white piles all around the perimeters of the buildings.

It wasn't always like that. There was a time when the stark white buildings stood proudly against the dark green grass. Frank smiled as he remembered the smell of fresh paint and newly cut grass. Work clothes and flowered dresses hung from a clothesline that stretched the length of the backyard. Frank turned to watch his small children as they played on a tire hanging from an oak tree across the driveway.

"Frank, supper's ready. Holler for the kids to come in."

Frank turned and looked over his shoulder. "Right away, Ida," he said.

He walked onto the back porch and opened the back door. He stepped outside and looked in the direction of the oak tree. The rope and tire were gone. Even the branch that supported it had fallen during a storm years ago.

Frank's face paled, and his smile disappeared. A gust of wind scattered the thin strands of hair on his head, and a discarded newspaper came to life, its pages spreading across the yard like ghosts in the wind.

"All those years ago," he muttered aloud, turning once again to the oak tree hoping to see that rope and tire. The fierce wind stung his tired eyes as Frank gazed across an open field. He stared into a river of memories until his heart could no longer take it. "All those years ago," he said again and turned back into the house.

3 THE NURSING HOME

The next morning brought a soft and gentle rain that helped to quench the unusually dry farmlands. The spring had been unseasonably dry, and any rain was a blessing to the farmers in the area.

Frank walked over to the sink and gazed out the window. The sky was overcast with dark, gray clouds that seemed to hang motionless just over the ground. Despite the need for rain, the cold, gray morning brought a sense of gloom and depression.

Frank needed to get out of the house. He needed to be with his friends. It was still early, but he decided to drive into town for breakfast anyway. Besides, he wanted to see if the new battery in his truck was working.

He walked across the backyard and climbed into his truck. With one turn of the key, the engine roared to life. Frank smiled as he backed the vehicle onto the road and started for town.

He had only traveled a short distance when he noticed a car just ahead pulled over to the side of the road. As he came closer, he could see that it was a woman, and she was in the process of changing a flat tire.

It was raining much harder now, and Frank could hardly see the road. He eased his truck over to the side and stopped just behind the parked car. Frank peered through the foggy window to see the woman vigorously pumping the handle of the jack raising one end of the car slowly into the air. He tried to see who the woman was, but she had her back to him as she knelt beside her car.

Frank wiped the inside of the windshield with his shirtsleeve. He could see that the car was high enough that the tire was no longer touching the ground. She continued to pump the jack until, suddenly, the vehicle eased forward until it finally fell off the jack and dropped to the ground.

Frank scrambled from his truck and ran over to the woman. "Are you all right?" he asked. The woman spun around at the sound of his voice. She pulled her rain-soaked hair from her eyes. "Oh, my God!" exclaimed Frank. "It's you, the new waitress!"

With both hands, the young woman wiped the rain from her face leaving streaks of mud across her forehead. Patches of mud clung to the knees of her white jeans bleeding small dark streams down the front of her legs. "You have an uncanny flair for the obvious, Mr. Watson," she barked.

"You remembered my name," noted Frank shielding his eyes with one of his hands.

"How could I forget the leader of the sandbox boys."

"Do you want some help?"

"It's because I'm a woman, isn't it?"

"What?"

"You don't think I can do this because I'm a woman. Isn't that right?"

"Hey, lady, don't get your panties all bunched up. I would have offered to help a man as well if he was as incompetent as you are."

"Incompetent? Who are you calling incompetent?"

Frank looked down at the flat tire that was now sinking in the mud. "I don't know, but unless I miss my guess, Sam Wilton's job as the only mechanic in town is still safe even after you came to town."

"Listen. I don't have time for this chitchat. I'm late for work, and I have a tire to change, so leave me alone," she said as she knelt on the ground in front of the car.

"Suit yourself," said Frank as he turned and walked back to his truck. He climbed into the cab and wiped his face with a rag. He cleaned the inside of the windshield once again and settled back to watch.

The young woman retrieved the jack from the mud and positioned it under the frame of the vehicle. She connected the handle and began to pump up and down. The car began to slowly rise and then suddenly stopped as the jack began to sink into the mud.

The woman stopped pumping the jack. She removed the handle and threw it into the ditch on the other side of the car. Frank leaned forward. He could see that she had her head lowered and was crying. For several moments, she remained on her hands and knees in the mud. Frank reached for the door handle but stopped short of opening the door.

Finally, she got to her feet and stood by her car watching the jack sink deeper into the mud. She turned and walked over to the driver's side of the truck parked behind her car. Frank slowly rolled down his window.

"Help me," she pleaded.

"Get in the truck," said Frank pointing to the passenger side. As she walked around to the other side of the truck, Frank got out and reached into the back of his truck. With both hands, he picked up a floor jack and walked over to her car. He positioned the device under the frame and began to pump the handle. Within seconds, the car was hoisted off the ground. Frank removed the five lug nuts and threw the lifeless tire into the back of his truck.

"I'll drop you off at work," said Frank climbing into the truck and closing the door. "Then, I'll take your tire over to Sam's Garage. He's not much of a mechanic, but he's all we got. Besides, it's only a flat tire. Even Sam can fix a flat."

"Why are you doing this for me?" she asked wiping her face with a rag.

"Why not?" Frank asked as he started the engine of his truck and put it into gear. "You needed help, didn't you?"

The young woman set the rag down on the seat and turned to watch her car as they pulled onto the road. "Thanks, Mr. Watson," she said turning back to Frank.

"Call me Frank."

"Pepper's my name," she said extending her hand. "Pepper Ledley."

Frank freed one hand from the steering wheel and took her hand. "Pepper. That's an unusual name."

"From the day I was born, my daddy always wanted me to be a little different from the rest. He always said that the world had enough females named Linda, Sue, and Kathy. I guess he figured that if he gave me a different name, I might be a little different."

"Well, are you?"

"Am I what?"

"Different. Are you a little different?"

"Maybe, a little," she said looking over at the man driving the truck. Frank smiled at her. "Well, more than just a little."

Silence followed. The only sound was the badly worn windshield wiper as it protested each trip across the glass.

"I'm sorry for the way I talked to you the other day," she said looking out the window. "That was wrong. I know that now. It's just that I'm trying to start a new life in your little town, and nothing seems to be going right. I guess I just wasn't in the mood for your friends and their little jokes."

"Don't pay any attention to that bunch of idiots. They're harmless and would do anything for you even if they didn't like you. That's just the way it is in a small town. Unfortunately, if you added up their combined I.Q., you probably wouldn't even need a calculator."

"Well, I probably shouldn't have been so sensitive."

"Don't worry about it," said Frank turning onto Main Street. "You couldn't hurt their feelings with an ax, probably because they don't have feelings." Frank brought the truck to a stop in front of the restaurant.

"What about my tire?" she asked.

"Let me borrow the keys to your car, and I'll take care of it." Pepper glanced at her purse that contained her keys and then back at Frank. "Don't worry. I won't steal your car."

"It's not that," she blurted. "It's the fact that you've done enough already."

"You're not from a small town, are you?"

"New York City."

"New York City? I don't think I've ever known someone who was actually from New York City," announced Frank. "Well, here in Springfield, we do things a little differently, so let me borrow your keys," he said extending an open hand in her direction.

Pepper dug into her purse and handed him the keys. "Thanks, again," she said as she climbed out of the truck.

Frank backed out of the parking space and drove the three blocks to Sam's Garage. "Good morning, Sam," said Frank as he dropped the tire on the ground in front of him.

"What the hell is good about it?" he snarled. "It's raining."

"You know, Sam, that's the kind of attitude that's bound to drive people away from your business."

"Jesus, Frank. You're in a good mood. Did your daily dose of Metamucil kick in?"

"You know, Sam, you've got to learn to relax. You take life too seriously."

Sam looked down at the tire lying at his feet. "Whose tire?"

"It belongs to the new waitress. You're going to fix it, and when I get back from breakfast, you and I are going to go put it on her car."

"Oh, so that explains your sudden good mood," said Sam. "You've got the hots for that pretty little thing, don't you, Frank?"

"God, you can be crude," Sam replied. "I'm just doing what every normal guy would do when someone needs help."

"Jesus, Frank. She's about half your age. Aren't there laws against things like that?"

"Just fix the tire, you moron," said Frank getting back into his truck. "I'll be back in a little bit."

It was still raining, and Frank decided to drive the three blocks to the restaurant. He parked his vehicle near the front door and walked inside.

"Morning, Frank," came a chorus of voices.

"Good morning, Gentlemen," he replied in a songlike voice. "And that includes you, George."

"My God," said George. "You're in a good mood."

"Aren't I always," Frank replied as he walked behind the counter to pour himself a cup of coffee.

"If I didn't know better, I'd say you got yourself laid," said George.

"Can't a fellow simply be in love with life?" asked Frank loud enough for the table to hear.

All conversation stopped. Everyone turned and stared at Frank. "Hey, I'm in a good mood," he said with a smile.

"Order your breakfast, Frank," said Willard Miller. "We have something serious to discuss."

"Even Willard is not going to spoil my day," he said as he turned to find a waitress.

"Good morning, Frank," said the waitress walking over to the table.

"Good morning, Pepper," he replied loudly. "My, you look lovely this morning."

Silence fell on the group of men as everyone stared at the end of the table.

"Let me see if I can remember. You want your eggs over medium and hash browns on the crispy side. Is that right?" she asked with a smile.

"Absolutely perfect!" he replied.

One of the men leaned towards the others sitting across the table. "There ain't no way that sweet young thing is going to have anything to do with that old turd," he mumbled to the others.

Pepper quickly glanced at that end of the table and then back at Frank. She picked up several dirty dishes and turned from the table. She had only taken two steps when she spun around. "By the way, thanks for last night, Frank," she cooed loudly. "You were just perfect," she added and walked away.

Silence fell on the room. One of the men had a forkful of food frozen in place only inches from his mouth. All eyes were focused on Frank. He sat up straight in his chair and turned to the men sitting at the long table. "Hey! Can you blame her?" he asked pointing to his face.

"I'm sure that someday we will all be interested in your sexual prowess, Frank, but today we have to talk about something more important," announced Willard.

Frank glanced at the man sitting at the end of the table. "What is it, Willard?" he asked. "What has got you so worked up?"

"I got to digging, and I found out who's trying to buy all the land around here," said Willard.

"And who might that be?" asked Frank.

"Some company that's based in Australia, of all places. They hired Sweeney to buy up five hundred acres to build an egg farm."

"An egg farm? What in the hell is an egg farm?" asked George.

"I know what it is," said Ben Sager. "There's one over in Jefferson County."

"That's funny," said Frank. "I've never heard about an egg farm anywhere around here."

"That's just it. Nobody knows much of anything about them," Ben replied as he filled his pipe with tobacco. "They quietly buy up parcels of land and build their egg farm out in the middle of nowhere."

"How do you know so much about them?" asked Frank.

"My brother Otis works there. He's been there over a year now. Old fool has no business working. He's almost as old as I am."

"See what I told you, Frank!" said Willard. "I knew that there was something going on!"

"Do you suppose you could call your brother sometime today, Ben?" asked Frank. "Maybe, he can give us some more information."

"You're not seriously thinking about selling your land, are you Frank?" asked Willard.

"Willard, I wouldn't sell my land if it was Jesus, himself, who was interested. I just want to find out more about these people. Besides, I'm not the only one you need to worry about. There are other farmers who might want to sell. Hell, there are two of them right here in this room."

Everyone turned to Ben Sager and Bob Howell. "Don't look at me like that." said Bob. "I'm in debt up to my ears from that worthless farm of mine, and I plan to listen to what the man has to say."

"Everybody just hold onto your water," said Ben. "I'll see what I can find out about this from my brother."

Just then, the waitress brought a plate of food to the table and set it in front of Frank. "There you go, Frank," she said with a smile. "I hope you enjoy your breakfast."

"I'm sure I will," he replied.

She walked halfway across the floor before she stopped and turned towards the table of men. "By the way, Frank," she said loudly. "Dinner at my house this Saturday night? Is that all right?"

"I wouldn't miss it for anything," he replied in the direction of his friends.

"Jesus, Frank," said George. "I wouldn't have believed it if I hadn't seen it with my own eyes."

"I told you once before, George," said Frank as he thrust his fork into a pile of hash browns. "I have this thing that women just can't resist."

"And just what the hell is this thing?" asked his friend leaning a little closer.

"I can't tell you, George. It's a secret," said Frank. "In fact, it's the best kept secret in the world. Nobody ever talks about it, but it's there. Everyone has it, but only a few know how to use it. Like I said. It's the greatest secret in the world."

"Come on, Frank," pleaded George. "I'm your best friend in the world. You have to tell me. You can't keep secrets like that from your best friend."

Frank took a bite from his toast and turned to his friend. "You know that if I let you in on this secret, I'll have to kill you later."

"Quit jerking me around, Frank. What is the secret to attracting women?"

Frank stuck another forkful of potatoes in his mouth and turned to his friend. "It's the eyes, George," he said confidently.

"The eyes? What are you talking about, Frank?"

"The eyes, George. People talk to one another every day without saying a word. They tell people things through their eyes, and they aren't talking to their brains, George. They're talking to their inner soul."

"You're so full of it, Frank."

"I'm telling you the truth, George. There's a special way of looking at a woman. If you do it right, you're looking straight into her soul. It's eye contact, George. There's a certain way of looking at a woman that says something to her."

"What are you saying to her?"

"George, from this point on, you're on your own. If you're lucky enough to make this kind of connection with a woman, the feelings that you share with her will be very personal. Just remember, George, that when this happens, you won't just be looking at her, you will be sharing a very special moment with this woman, and it will magically happen through the eyes."

"Sounds kind of weird, Frank," said George. "Do you suppose I can do it?"

"Once you know the secret, anybody can do it," said Frank setting his fork on his empty plate.

"Thanks, Frank," said his friend staring out the window. "I can't wait to try it."

"Good luck," said Frank as he picked up his bill and walked to the register.

"That will be $3.85," said Rackets as he hit the keys on the machine.

"Hey, Rackets," said Frank handing him a five-dollar bill. "You picked a winner for a waitress this time. That new girl is really good at her job."

"Yeah, and she's got a great looking ass," said Rackets handing him his change.

"You know, Rackets," said Frank as he thrust the coins into his pocket. "Having spent these few moments with you has taught me two things."

"Yeah, and what is that, Frank?"

"I now know why there are so many women in the world who hate men, and I also know why you're still single."

Frank turned and started for the front door. He stopped by his empty chair and drained the last of the coffee that remained in his cup. "Have a good day, George," he said.

"Same to you, old friend," said George. Frank returned the cup to the table and walked away. "Frank, you dropped a dollar on the table!" shouted George waving the bill in the air.

"Just leave it," he said quietly and walked away.

Moments later, Frank pulled into the parking lot of Sam Wilton's Garage. The rain had ended by now, and rays of sunlight pierced through the dark clouds lighting the Earth below.

"Did you get that tire fixed?" asked Frank.

"It holds air, but I don't know for how long," Sam replied. From the size of the hole, she must have run over something mighty big. Besides, patchin' that tire was just a waste of time."

"Why is that?" asked Frank walking over to Sam's truck.

"That tire is slicker than a baby's butt," Sam replied climbing into the driver's side of his truck. "The patch I put on it is worth more than the tire."

The two men drove to the abandoned car and within minutes had the patched tire remounted. Frank drove the car into town and parked it in front of the restaurant. He removed the keys from the ignition and entered the restaurant. By that time, Ben Sager and Willard Miller were the only two still sitting at the long table. They stopped their conversation and stared as

Frank walked over to the waitress holding a set of keys in his outstretched hand.

"Your tire is fixed, and your car is parked right outside the door," he announced as he handed her the keys.

"Thanks, Frank," she said taking the keys. "Thank you very much. I don't know what I would have done without you." She leaned forward and kissed him on the cheek and gave a quick hug.

Frank was frozen in place, his hands at his sides. "No problem. My pleasure. You bet 'cha," he muttered as she disappeared into the kitchen. He turned and walked across the floor towards the front door, the two men at the table watching intently. He let himself out the front door and turned onto the sidewalk that led to Sam's Garage.

"Frank! Over here, Frank!" shouted Sam who had been waiting in his truck. He shifted into first gear and eased out the clutch following slowly behind the man on the sidewalk. "Frank, get in the truck! I'll give you a ride!" Frank said nothing. "Wake up, Frank!" he shouted out the window of his vehicle. Sam stared at the man blindly walking down the sidewalk and finally drove off leaving him behind.

Moments later, Sam watched as Frank walked across the front of his shop in the direction of his own truck. "Frank, you owe me five dollars for fixing that flat." The man opened the door of his truck and climbed in. "Frank, who's going to pay me five bucks?" The man started the engine and drove from the parking lot and onto Main Street. "Have a nice day," muttered Sam as he watched the faded red truck drive out of sight.

It was just after nine o'clock when Frank pulled into the driveway of his house and parked in front of his garage. He had just stepped into the kitchen when the back door flew open.

"Jesus, Frank, is it true?" asked Toad closing the door behind her.

"Is what true?"

"My God, Frank, you're the talk of the town."

"Now, what did I do?"

"It's more like what haven't you done, Frank," said Toad walking across the kitchen towards the coffee maker. They say that you've already shacked up with the new waitress. You were seen kissing her in public and on the lips, and you even left a tip. Now, I'd say things are getting pretty serious, Mr. Watson."

"You know, Toad. It's too bad that your information isn't as accurate as it is expedient. Yes, she gave me a kiss, but it was on the cheek. She was just thanking me for changing her flat tire."

"What about the rumor that you and her have already been horizontal together?"

"That was nothing," said Frank taking a seat at the kitchen table. "We were just playing a little joke on the other guys."

Toad finished preparing the coffee and sat down across from Frank. "So, what are you telling me, Frank? Are you telling me that you're not interested in this woman?"

"I don't know, Toad," he said folding his hands together. I really don't know what to do. It's been two years since Ida died, and I still love her as much as the first day I met her. I just can't seem to let her go, Toad."

"You know, Frank, I never told you or anybody else, but all those years that I knew Ida I was jealous of her." Frank stared at the woman sitting before him with a puzzled look. "I always wanted a relationship with a man like she had with you. There were so many things about you two that I dearly loved and will probably never forget. I remember how you never forgot any of the holidays. No matter which one it was, you never forgot. Even on Ida's birthday, you always baked her a cake. I know it sounds silly for me to remember that, but it just seemed so special. You were always busy with the farm at that time of the year, and you didn't know the first thing about boiling water, and, yet, she always had a homemade cake for every birthday."

"Some of those cakes didn't turn out so good."

"It didn't matter, Frank. The important thing was that you loved her enough to try."

"I suppose you're right."

Toad poured two cups of coffee and returned to her seat. "The thing I envied the most, Frank, was the fact that even in your later years, you still held hands. I think that's the best part of all. In my mind, there is nothing sweeter than a man who has been married as long as you and still wants to tell the world that he loves his wife by holding her hand."

"Toad, I appreciate your kind words, but what's this have to do with my problem?"

"You and Ida had something special, Frank. Everyone who ever knew you was certain of that. Nobody expects you to stop loving that woman who was a part of your life for over forty years, but we do expect you to get on with your life."

"It just doesn't seem right, Toad."

"Frank, you and I both know that if there was anyone who was destined to go to heaven, it was Ida. I, personally, can only hope that I'll see her when my time comes, but there's no question about Ida. If you ask me, Frank, she's watching over you right now, and she most likely sent this woman into your life to give you a new start. Jesus, Frank, take this opportunity and run with it."

"Well, that's all well and good, but how do I know if she's interested?"

"From what I hear, you have a date with her Saturday night. I'd say that was a pretty good sign."

"That's just it. I don't know if she was serious or was just kidding around.

"I'd say you'd better find out. By the way, Frank, where does she live?"

"She's renting a room from Warren Hainey."

A broad grin spread across Toad's face. "She has invited you to dinner out there?"

"What's wrong with that?"

"Frank, that place should have fallen down years ago, and they say that Warren is getting worse every day."

"Worse about what?"

"His mind, Frank. When's the last time you've seen him? He's not sure what planet he's on let alone what day it is. Poor old Irma is at her wit's end trying to take care of him."

"Someday, you have to tell me how you find out about all this stuff. The government should hire you for spy work or something."

"Don't you worry about my sources of information. I'd say your biggest concern right now is to find out if this woman was serious about Saturday night," said Toad getting to her feet.

"Why don't you go in there early tomorrow morning before your idiot friends get there, and you might have a chance to talk to her." She started for the door. "Right now, I've got to be going."

Frank hurried across the room and opened the door for his friend. "Thanks, Toad, for helping me," he said staring out the open door. "I know I can be a pain in the ass sometimes, but I'm grateful that I have you for a friend."

"That's quite all right, Frank. I just want you to be happy. Hell, I should have married you before Ida did," she said walking out the door.

"Well, I'm available now," he called out the door.

"No thanks, Frank," she shouted over her shoulder. "You're too old for a mature and robust woman like me. I'll keep searching for an eighteen-year-old who can keep up."

৪৩ ৪৩ ৪৩

It was late afternoon when the faded red truck parked in front of the nursing home. Frank signed in at the front desk and made his way down the hallway that led to his father's room. He grimaced at the pungent odors that seemed to fill the entire building.

Halfway down the hall, Frank was stopped by several residents whose wheelchairs had locked together creating a barrier that stretched from wall-to-wall. Frank studied the situation. There was no break in the blockade for him to pass, and every one of the residents involved was slumped over deep in sleep. He pulled on one of the chairs hoping to unlock the wheels.

Suddenly, Frank felt someone grab his arm near the wrist. Icy, cold fingers wrapped around his wrist in a grip that nearly cut off his blood. Frank turned to see that it was Bess, one of the few residents who could walk.

"Let go of me!" shouted Frank as he jerked on one of the wheelchairs with his free hand.

"Get me out of here," she shouted, her grip tightening. The panic-struck man jerked again on the wheelchair entangling the wheels even more. "You must take me home with you!" she screamed.

"You've got to let me go!" shouted Frank as he tried to pry her fingers from his wrist. By now, the loud commotion had awakened the others. A man next to Frank grabbed him by the leg. Frank panicked. He snapped his arm downward freeing himself from the woman's grip. With both hands, he pulled the wheelchair backwards until it freed itself from the others. The woman stepped closer, her body touching his.

Frank pulled the man's hand from his leg and stepped through the opening. A chorus of screams filled the hallway as Frank raced towards his father's room.

"Hi, Pop," greeted Frank panting profusely. "How are you doing today?"

"Hi there, Tough Guy," he replied with a smile. "I'm fine. How are you?"

"I'm real good, Dad," he replied shaking his hand. "This must be a good day for you. You're even smiling."

"What are you talking about? I'm always smiling."

"If you're such a hot shot, what's my name?"

"You're Frank, the mailman's son."

"I know better, Pop," he said taking a seat next to his father's bed. "I inherited the same cranky disposition that you have. Thank God, I got Mom's good looks though."

"So, what brings you to this house of horrors?"

"Well, something's come up in my life, Dad, and I need to ask you a question. After Mom died, did you ever date anyone else?"

"Nope. Not me," he said loudly shifting his weight in bed. "You know, they broke the mold after they made your mother. I knew there would never be anyone good enough to replace her. That's not to say that I didn't have my chances, you understand. More than one lady has glanced in my direction, let me tell you. Why do you ask, anyhow?"

"Something has come up, and I might just have the chance to take out a woman half my age."

"Does she have big hooters?"

"Excuse me!"

"Breasts, Son. Does she have big breasts?"

"I don't know, Dad. I guess I just didn't notice."

"Jesus, Son, you're getting old!"

"The size of her breasts is not my problem. My problem is that it's only been two years since Ida died."

"Who the hell's Ida?"

"Come on, Dad. Ida Watson, my wife and your daughter-in-law for over forty years."

"Oh, yes. Ida. How's she doing?"

"She's dead Pop!"

"I'm sorry to hear that, Son. So, what's the problem?"

"I don't know, Pop. It just doesn't seem right to date someone else. I feel like I'm being unfaithful to that woman whom I still deeply love."

"That's a bunch of crap, Son. If you have a chance for a little happiness, go for it!" shouted the old man. "Especially, if you think you might get laid."

"Dad!"

"And you say this girl's name is Ida? That's strange. I once had a daughter-in-law by that name."

Frank stared at his father for a moment. Before he could respond, he heard the sound of slippers sliding across the tile floor. "Oh Christ!" he shouted as he jumped from his chair. Bess walked slowly across the room towards the two men babbling incoherently.

"What's wrong?" asked the old man.

"It's that woman," he said pointing across the room. "She scares the crap out of me."

"Bess!" shouted Frank's father. The old woman stopped. "I told you once before that I don't want you in here. Now, get the hell out of here!" She stood in the middle of the room staring at the wall. "Go on and get out of here!" The old woman turned and shuffled out the door.

"Jesus, Dad, I thought the days of your protecting me were long gone."

"You just need to have a way with women like I do."

"Well, Dad, I need to be going," he said sliding the chair back against the wall, "but first let me ask you my favorite question."

"What question is that?"

"Hopefully, today will be the day. I don't think I've ever seen you so alert."

"So, ask the question!"

"Tell me, Pop, what did you get me for my sixteenth birthday?"

"I don't know, Son, but for your next birthday, I hope you get laid. It might relax you a bit."

"Got to go, Dad," said Frank walking towards the door. "See you soon."

"Good bye, son," was the faint reply.

₮ ₮ ₮

Bob's Cafe had just opened for the day when a tall, middle aged man walked through the front door.

"Morning, Frank," said Rackets easing himself into his favorite booth. "Fall out of bed this morning?"

"Just one of those mornings when I couldn't wait to get at the delicious food served in this fine establishment," said Frank pouring himself a cup of coffee.

"Somehow, I get the feeling that you just gave me a shot," said Rackets sipping his own coffee.

"Nothing slips by you, my friend."

"Are you going to want some breakfast, Frank, or are you waiting for your misfit friends?"

Frank sat straight in his chair and lightly patted his stomach with both hands. "I think I'd like to eat right now," he said. "For some reason, I seem to have an appetite this morning."

"Pepper!" shouted Rackets towards the kitchen. "You've got a customer!"

Moments later, the young woman appeared from the back room. "Morning, Frank," she smiled. "How are you this morning?"

"I'm fine. How are you?"

"Never better," she replied.

Frank fell silent as he stared at the woman standing before him. He leaned back on his chair tipping it back on two legs. He glanced over at the corner booth to find Rackets with a pencil bent over a piece of paper.

"How's that tire doing?" he asked. "Is it still holding air?"

"Oh, it's fine, Frank," she replied. "It's doing just fine." Silence followed. "Would you like some breakfast?"

"Sure. That sounds great."

"Would you like the usual?"

"Sure," he replied holding out a pointed finger.

"Was there something else?"

Once again, Frank glanced over at Rackets and then to the woman standing in front of him. "I need to ask you a question."

"Sure. What is it?"

"The other day when we were playing around with the guys, you said something about Saturday night."

"I sure did."

"I was just wondering if you were still playing around when you said it?"

"Never been more serious."

"Really?" Frank smiled.

"Really."

"You know that you don't have to pay me back for fixing your tire."

"I'm not paying you back for fixing my tire."

"Really?"

"Really."

Frank found that he now had a smile on his face that would not go away even when he spoke. "What time should I be there?"

"Six o'clock and don't be late. The Hainey's like to go to bed early."

"I'll be there."

"Now, how 'bout that breakfast?"

"Skip it," said Frank pulling a dollar bill from his pocket. "I have to be going."

"Is everything all right?"

"Everything is fine. It's just that if I start right now, I might be able to clean myself up good enough for Saturday night."

"See you, Frank," she said with a smile. Rackets looked up to see the man walking out of the restaurant.

"Good bye, Pepper," he called over his shoulder. "Have a great day, Rackets," he added.

4 IDA

Saturday morning dawned in a spectacle of fiery reds and oranges that seemed to stretch like fingers across the sky. Unable to sleep, Frank was up early to face the new day.

It was near ten o'clock in the morning when the back door opened and closed. Toad stepped just inside and stopped to watch a man as he searched frantically through kitchen cupboards.

"What are you looking for, Frank?"

"My shoe brush, for Christ sakes," he replied opening another door. "I can't find it anywhere."

"Jesus, Frank, why are you in such a stew over a shoe brush?"

"I'm having dinner with Pepper tonight, and my shoes look like I walked through a cow pie."

"Oh, that's right," said Toad with a smile. "You have a date tonight, don't you Frank?"

"It's not a date," he snapped. "She's just fixing the Hainey's and me dinner. That's all."

"Call it what you will, Frank, but in my book, you've got a date. Now, what did this brush look like?" she asked as she opened a closet.

"It was a beautiful oak handle shoe brush that Ida gave to me on our last Christmas together. It even has my name on it with the date of that Christmas Day. Jesus, I dearly love that thing."

"Hold on, Frank," said Toad as she searched the closet. "We'll find it. By the way, when did you last use it?"

"I polish my shoes every Saturday out there on that back porch, and I always leave it out there by the back door."

"Did you check out there?"

"Christ, Toad! I only look stupid! Sure, I looked out there!"

"Good God, Frank," said Toad walking across the kitchen. "Have you had anything to eat this morning? You always get this way when you're hungry."

"I'm too damn nervous to eat. Besides, I need to find that brush."

"Sit down, Frank," she said dipping a measuring spoon into a can of coffee. "We'll find your shoe brush, but right now, you need to take a break and drink a cup of coffee."

"Maybe, you're right," he said as he sat down at the kitchen table. "I just can't believe that I'm going to see a woman socially."

"What's so hard to believe?" she asked as she sat down across from him.

"Jesus Christ, Toad, the last time I dated, Eisenhower was president, Aids was something you did to help someone else, and Rap was something you did on the front door. I'm not even sure what men and women do with each other when they're alone."

"Quit worrying, Frank. Everything will be just fine. In the first place, it's just dinner. You're not expected to go down on one knee on your first date. Besides, if this young friend of yours is crazy about a man of your age, she'll probably steal Warren away from Irma before you even get to dessert."

"Thanks, Toad, I knew I could depend on you for some of your homespun advice."

"Relax, Frank," she said pouring coffee into two cups. "You'll do just fine. Just be yourself, and you'll charm the pants off her. Well, so to speak." She set the two cups on the table and returned to her seat. "I'm happy to see that you're finally able to deal with the memory of Ida."

"That's just it," he said taking a sip from his coffee. "I haven't dealt with that. I feel like I'm cheating on her."

"She's dead, Frank. It's not considered cheating when your spouse has died."

Silence followed as Frank stared out the window. He picked up his cup of coffee and held it for several moments as if he had forgotten it was there. "I know she's gone," he said with a heavy voice. "I tell myself that every day. I think I've finally learned to believe that, but then there are times when I still can't believe it. There are times when I don't think I can take it anymore. My heart aches for her so much sometimes that I can't stand it."

Toad reached across the table and laid her hand on his. "I'm sorry, Frank," she said softly.

"You know, Toad, there are times when I can walk into this kitchen and close my eyes, and I can still smell her. I can smell the cookies that she's baking. I can smell her hair, a light touch of perfume, everything that was her. My God, it's almost as if she were here. I can't help it that I miss her so much. To me, she's still my wife. Nothing's changed. I can't stop loving her."

"No one ever expected you to stop loving her, Frank."

"Then, how could I possibly see another woman if I still love my wife? It seems so wrong, like I'm being unfaithful."

Toad tightened her grip on Frank's hand. "Frank, you feel her presence, don't you?"

"What do you mean?"

"I mean that there are times that you can feel that she is here in this room with you."

"Yes, how did you know?"

"I believe that we all have guardian angels, and I have no doubt that Ida is yours."

Frank turned to his friend. "It's funny and I can't explain it, but some days I can feel her. I know as certain as anything that she's here. It's like a presence. I just can't see her. You know, the sad thing about life and the living is that we often take for granted those whom we love, and only after they're gone do we realize what we had. You know, Toad, I'd give everything I have just to sit down at that table for a Sunday dinner with all my kids and Ida just one more time." Toad reached for a tissue to wipe away the tears that were now flowing down her face. "My God, how wrong could I have been all those years ago. I thought I knew what was important. I didn't have a clue. I had no idea how short life really is. I wasted so much time. If I could only do it over. If I could only see her face one more time."

"Frank, you know what you need to do. You've come this far. It's time, and you know it."

"I can't do it."

"I'll be with you, Frank. You've got to do it though. It's time."

"I don't know whether I can do it or not. It's been over two years."

"Come on, Frank," she said getting to her feet.

Frank got up from his chair and walked across the kitchen. He stopped halfway into the living room as he stared at the bedroom door. Suddenly, he could see her lifeless body lying in their bed. The coffee cup from which she had been drinking lay shattered on the floor beside the bed, its contents splattered on the small white rug.

Frank walked slowly across the room and stopped just in front of the door, his hand only inches from it. He could see her stretching in front of the open window of their bedroom. The morning sunlight poured over her like a spring shower. A gentle breeze fluttered her nightgown and wrapped it tightly against her, revealing her womanly charm.

Frank reached for the door handle. He turned to his friend who was standing near him. She gave him a reassuring nod and a smile. He turned the handle and swung the door open. A musty smelling whirlwind seemed to escape from the darkened room.

Frank stood in the doorway staring at the room's contents. Everything was as they left it. Nothing had been disturbed since that day. The shade on the window was drawn, and it was difficult to see. He stepped into the room and began to breathe in the air in deep gulps.

"Are you all right, Frank?" asked Toad.

"Her last breath is somewhere in this room," he said filling his lungs one more time.

Toad walked past him to the window on the other side of the room. She lifted the shade, unlocked the window and raised it as well. Frank stared at the open window and the dusty curtains as they lightly danced in the soft breeze. It was as if they had come to life in the gentle wind.

Frank was surprised. For the past two years, he had blamed this room for taking Ida away from him. Yet, in the morning light, this room seemed so innocent, not the evil place that he imagined.

He scanned the room, his eyes falling onto the small white rug at the side of the bed. The stains were still there. He stared at the mocha colored spots and remembered that day. She hadn't felt good all morning and wanted a cup of coffee. She sat up in bed as he delivered the hot beverage to her in her favorite china cup. "You're so good to me," she smiled. "I should be serving you in bed."

"Don't be silly," he muttered. "You're the one who doesn't feel good."

"In all the years we've been married, I never once served you anything in bed, she said sipping her coffee. "For that, I'm sorry."

"I never gave it a thought."

"You work so hard, Frank, and everyone needs to be pampered once in a while. I promise when I feel better I will serve you the biggest and best breakfast you ever had."

"I'm going to hold you that promise, Ida."

"Frank, your coffee is good but just a little too warm. Could you bring me an ice cube please?"

"Sure, Ida. I'll be right back."

A gust of wind blew through the room sending a cloud of dust swirling across the floor. Frank walked across the room and sat on Ida's side. The bed groaned in protest. He pulled back the comforter and with one hand stroked the cool sheets where she had last rested. He had wanted to do this for so long. He had often dreamed of caressing that special spot. His hand seemed to drink in the coolness of the sheets.

Frank glanced up at the soft pillow at the head of the bed. He stared at the small valley in its center that once cradled her head. His eyes blurred with the tears of the last two years.

He gently slipped both hands under the down-filled treasure and pulled it near him. This was her favorite pillow and she used it for many years. He hoped that it had been preserved in that sealed room for the last two years. He lowered his face until he was nearly touching it and inhaled deeply, filling his lungs with the soft fragrance that seemed to fill the air.

"She's here," he said turning to Toad. "I can feel it. She's here in this room."

"How can you tell, Frank?"

"I know that I can't see her, but she's here in this room with us. I lived with that woman for over forty years, and I can feel her presence right now." Frank returned the pillow to its place at the head of the bed. "I know it sounds crazy, but she's real close to us right now. I can feel it."

Toad sat on a wooden chair on the other side of the bed. "Are you all right, Frank?"

Frank turned and scanned the room. There had to be a reason for this overwhelming feeling that he was experiencing. Over the past two years he had felt her presence, but it was never like this.

His eyes finally stopped at the nightstand on her side of the bed. There laid a variety of personal effects that had belonged to Ida. The book that she was reading, her wedding ring, a needle and thread, and a hairbrush were scattered on the stand just as she had left them.

Frank picked up the hairbrush and studied it carefully. It was full of long tresses of golden hair that had once belonged to that woman of his eternal dreams. He carefully untangled the delicate strands from the brush one by one in such a manner that preserved them in a near pristine condition. He carefully placed the valuable find in his shirt pocket and returned the brush to its position on the nightstand.

"It's almost as if I was able to touch her once again," he said turning to his friend. Just then, his eyes caught sight of something on the nightstand next to Toad. It was the nightstand that had served his needs for so many years, and something was setting on top of it. It seemed so strange to Frank since he had always made a point to keep it empty and uncluttered.

"Toad, what is that next to you," he said pointing at the small object.

Toad picked up the object and studied it for a moment. "It's a shoe brush, Frank. In fact, it's the one you've been looking for because it has your name and the date of that Christmas of two years ago. Frank, it looks like you simply forgot that you left it in here."

"Let me see that," he said taking the brush from his friend. He studied it for several moments and then looked up at Toad. This is it, all right. This is the brush that I have been using every Saturday night for the last two years. There's no doubt of that, but the problem is that I haven't been in this room in two years. The two people stared at the brush for several moments in an almost trance like state, got up from the bed, and left the room.

Around six o'clock Frank slipped on his brown tweed sport coat and straightened his tie as he peered into the mirror in the front vestibule. He glanced down at the mirror finish on his shoes and smiled to himself.

Frank backed the truck out of the drive and onto the road. The Hainey farm was less than a mile down the road, and in just moments, Frank was pulling into their stone drive. He turned off his engine and stared at the old and decadent house and its surrounding buildings. He had only driven by this place, hardly giving any notice, and it had been years since he had actually stopped and visited these old and venerable friends of his. It was obvious that there had been no repair or upkeep to this farm in years. It was as if the farm was slowly dying with its occupants.

Frank got out of his truck and walked around to the front of the house. The roof on the house needed repair, and the paint was all but gone from the outside. The front door opened before he even reached the steps of the porch.

"Good evening, Mr. Watson," came a voice through the dark screen door.

"Good evening, Pepper," was his reply as he let himself through the door. "Something smells good."

"It's my specialty, fried chicken," she said. "You're just in time. We were just sitting down. Have a seat at the table."

Frank entered the dining room to find Warren and Irma sitting at opposite ends of a long table loaded with bowls of food and adorned with a centerpiece and candles. Irma was wearing a new dress, and Warren his best suit. Frank stared at Warren since that was the first time he could remember seeing him wearing one other than the occasional funeral that he would attend. "Good evening, folks," said Frank pulling out a chair on one side of the table.

"Good evening, Frank," said Irma. "My, don't you look nice."

"Well, thanks, Irma. You look..."

"Frank, what the hell are you doing here?" asked Warren.

"I was invited over for dinner."

"Well, good. While you're here, you might as well have dinner with us," he said passing a bowl of chicken to the guest.

Frank turned to Irma who was glaring at her husband from across the room. Pepper removed her apron and took a seat across from Frank. "My, everything looks and smells so good," he said with a smile.

"I can't remember when we've had a dinner this nice," said Irma passing a bowl to Pepper.

Frank finished pouring gravy on his mashed potatoes and began to eat his meal. "My God, this chicken is as good as it smells," he said taking a bite from the drumstick in his hands.

"Where the hell is Ida?" asked Warren in a loud voice. "You should have brought her with you."

"Ida passed away."

"What?"

Irma put down her fork and leaned over the table. "Ida died two years ago, Warren!" she shouted.

"Oh," he muttered and took another bite of his food. "Does she know that you're over here visiting this young thing? I don't think she would approve, Frank."

Frank turned again to Irma who was scowling at her husband. She picked up her fork and began to eat again. Silence fell as the four people vigorously attacked their dinner. "What kind of crop did you put in this spring, Frank? Wheat? Corn? Oats?"

"I'm retired, Warren. I don't do any farming anymore."

"What?"

"He says he's retired!" shouted Irma.

"Retired! Holy Christ, Frank, you're just a kid. You must be getting lazy," he said without looking up.

Frank said nothing. Silence returned as everyone continued with their meal.

"So, Frank," said Irma. "I hear someone is interested in your farm. Do you think you'll be selling out?"

"Oh, I don't think so, Irma. You see, I..."

"So, tell me, Frank," said Warren in a loud voice. "Is Ida going to enter another one of her rhubarb pies in the county fair this year? Best goddamn pie I ever tasted."

"Ida is gone," said Frank.

"What?"

"Ida is dead, Warren!" he shouted.

Pepper kicked Frank under the table. "Be nice," she said softly with a smile.

"I know. I know."

"He's a good man," she said quietly. "He can't help it that he can't hear all the time."

"What are you two talking about?" barked Warren. "You're making fun of me, aren't you? Right here in my own house, you two snotty little kids are making fun of me."

"Settle down, Warren," said his wife.

"Do you think it's funny that I can't hear all the time? Do you think I like being old? Do you think it's fun when your whole body aches so bad that you don't think you can stand it another day? Do you think it's funny that I have to wear a diaper, and I have to have my wife tie my goddamn shoes? Trust me, young man, if you should be so lucky to live to my age, you'll find that there are a lot less things in the world to laugh at."

Silence fell on the room as they finished eating dinner. On one occasion, Frank exchanged glances with Pepper, but nothing was said. Frank finished just ahead of the others and pushed his chair back from the table. He pulled his pipe from his pocket and began to load it with soft, aromatic tobacco from a zippered pouch. Warren stopped eating and stared at the man. He lightly tamped the tobacco into the bowl of his pipe and closed the pouch. Warren set his fork on his empty plate and turned slightly to watch the activity next to him. Frank struck a match and let it dance over the bowl of the pipe puffing vigorously to ignite the contents. Within moments, he could extinguish the match as the top of the tobacco glowed a bright red.

Warren watched intently as small billows of smoke rose majestically into the air. "Jesus, Frank," said Warren. "I wish you wouldn't do that. I got a lung condition, and that just seems to make it worse."

Frank pulled the pipe from his mouth and held it in midair. He looked across the table at Pepper with a wide-eyed expression and then at Irma.

"Let's all go sit in the living room," announced Irma getting to her feet. The others quietly got to their feet and followed the woman into the next room. Warren eased himself into his soft vinyl chair and pushed it back into a reclining position. Irma took her place next to her husband on a straight-back kitchen chair. The only place left to sit was a tattered old sofa that had over twenty decorative throw pillows piled on one end. The man and woman sat down at the other end. It was quiet in the room. The only sound was the deep ticking from a mantle clock that was setting on the television.

"That was a good dinner," said Frank turning slightly towards the woman sitting next to him. "You are a good cook."

"Well, thank you, sir," she replied. "I'm glad that you..."

"How's your dad doing, Frank?" blurted Warren.

"He's fine," Frank replied. "He's doing just fine."

"Tell him I want him to combine my wheat this year. I'll pay him good money."

"Dad's in a nursing home, Warren."

"What?"

"Dad's in a nursing home!" shouted Frank. "You'll have to get someone else to do the work."

"Ah, that figures," Warren mumbled. "Never could depend on that man." Frank turned to protest his last remark when suddenly the man shouted, "What the hell time is it, Irma?"

"It's almost seven o'clock."

"Jesus Christ! Turn on the goddamn television! Lawrence Welk is on!" Irma scrambled to her feet and turned the knob on the set. Within seconds, the TV roared to life, its volume level set for everyone in town to hear. "Turn it up, Irma," he said. "We got company."

Frank leaned over and shouted in Pepper's ear, "Any louder, and Lawrence, himself, will sit up in his grave."

Within ten minutes, Frank glanced over to see both Warren and Irma with their heads bent over. He nudged Pepper in the arm and pointed at their hosts. Despite the high volume of the television, Frank could still hear a raucous noise as Warren began to snore.

Frank got up from the sofa and held out his hand to the woman still sitting. With his help, she lifted herself from the couch, and the two people walked out on the front porch.

"I'd like to stay and finish that show, but I already know how it ends," said Frank leaning on the porch banister.

"Sorry about the television in there," said Pepper sitting on the porch swing across from him.

"Don't give it another thought," said Frank. "Warren has been like that ever since I can remember. I swear he was born deaf."

"He's certainly a colorful person."

"You know, Pepper," said Frank staring at the floor. "I really appreciate you having me over tonight. That was the best home cooked meal I've had in a long time, but I still have to wonder why. Why would you invite an old man like me over? You know I'm old enough to be your father."

"Is the age thing that important to you?"

"No. I'm just wondering how you could be interested in an old turd like me."

Pepper leaned back in the swing and gently put it in motion. "When I was a little girl, I spent a lot of time with my grandmother. I loved that woman very much. My own mother worked all the time since my father left us when I was little, so I spent much of my time with Grandma Izzy. Most of what I know today I learned from that woman.

One day, I asked her about my grandfather. I had heard that he had been gone for a long time, and it only seemed natural to ask of his fate. She told me that he died of cancer a year after they were married. I told her how sorry I was and that it was too bad that she didn't know of his condition before they were married, and she told me that she knew that he only had a short time to live. I was so dumfounded that I could hardly speak. The very idea that someone would marry another person knowing full well that they would soon die was too much for me. I guess I was only nine or ten years old. I thought I knew everything there was to know, but I still would lend an ear to Grandma Izzy. So, I asked her the obvious question. I asked her why she would marry a man who only had months to live. Do you know what she said?" Frank gave a gentle shake of his head. "She told me that she would rather have a year of happiness with the man she loves than a lifetime of wondering what might have been."

"She sounds like a wonderful woman."

"I saw her the day before she died. I could tell something was wrong. She just didn't seem herself. She seemed distant when I talked with her almost like she knew something. Now, when I look back, I like to think she was communicating with someone who was preparing her. Anyway, I wanted to say something to her to cheer her up. I wanted to say the right thing that would make her happy, so I told her that I was sure that she had much happiness in her future. You know, it was like giving a card to someone to help them get over a death in the family or the mumps or something. Well, anyway, she turned to me and looked me straight in the eyes. I'll never forget that day as long as I live. She looked at me with eyes that seemed to smile with the knowledge of something special and said that she was about to embark on a journey that would give her an eternity of happiness. I didn't know what she meant at the time, but I guess the way she said it seem to haunt me. Somehow, I knew at the time that what she said was important and that I should make every effort to remember it just as she said it."

Scott Fields

"Do you think she knew that she was about to die?"

"Oh, I'm quite sure of it. In fact, I am quite certain that on that last day of her life, she knew that she would soon be reunited with that man with whom she had spent so little time. To this day, that look on her face still haunts me. She knew. She knew where she was going on that journey. She had the look of inner peace, and I think she knew more than she was permitted to tell me."

Silence followed as Frank shifted his weight on the railing of the porch. "Whatever happened to your mother?"

"She lives back home in New York. She lives alone and collects her pension."

"How do you get along with her?"

"I call her on Thanksgiving and Christmas. That's about it."

Silence returned to the couple until finally Frank got to his feet. "I need to be going," he said and walked over to the front steps.

"I hope I didn't bore you too much with my childhood stories," she said getting to her feet.

"Quite the contrary," he said. "I found it to be a very interesting story. In fact, I had a great time."

Pepper stopped directly in front of the man. "When will I see you again, Mr. Watson?" she asked with a smile.

"I was wondering if you have a day off this next week."

"I'm off on Wednesday."

"Can you come over to my place around noon?"

"I'll be there."

Moments passed as they stared at each other. Frank slightly bent his head as if he was about to kiss her, and she raised up on her toes. He straightened back up and thrust out his hand. She lowered herself and took his hand with a smile.

"See you Monday morning?" asked Frank slowly shaking her hand.

"Bright and early," she replied staring into the man's eyes. She gave him a smile that suggested that it would be all right for him to kiss her.

Frank stared into her smiling eyes for several moments and then turned and walked away. "Say good night to the Hainey's for me," he called out and drove away in his truck.

5 THE BARN

Monday morning ushered in a bright, sunlit day that seemed to promise good things were just ahead. Frank opened the front door of the small cafe and headed for the coffee in the back. "Good morning, my friends," he announced with a wave of his hand.

"Good morning, Frank," came a few scattered voices.

"And isn't it a lovely morning?" he asked carrying his coffee to the table.

"Jesus, Frank," came a voice at the other end of the table. "I liked you more when you weren't getting any."

"Frank, you were right," said George excitedly grabbing him by the arm.

"Right about what?" he asked taking his seat.

"That eye contact stuff with women. I think it worked for me."

"Well, what happened?" asked Frank slowly stirring his coffee.

"You know Clara Butts who runs the cash register over at the Cash and Carry?"

"Clara Butts? Did you say Clara Butts, George?" asked Frank beginning to laugh. "Clara Butts weighs over three hundred pounds."

"Hey, Clara has a glandular condition. That's all. She can't help it."

"Tell me how she's big-boned too."

"Well, she is a big-boned girl."

"George, that isn't a bone hanging over her belt, and if her butt was any bigger, she'd need a license plate on it."

"She's not that bad."

"Go on and tell me what happened."

"Well, last Saturday, I went into the Cash and Carry to pick up some fixings for sandwiches. I like sandwiches for my lunches, you know, and they had some of that new kind of bologna on sale. Frank, have you tried that new kind that doesn't have hardly any fat in it? They call it light bologna or low fat. I'm not sure which. Do you know, Frank?"

"Get to the point, George!" shouted his friend sipping from his coffee.

"What point are you talking about, Frank? I told you I wasn't sure what they call that kind of bologna."

"George, tell me about Clara Butts and the eye contact thing."

"Oh, yeah. Clara Butts. I almost forgot. Well, anyway, I took my stuff up to the register and laid it down in front of her. There wasn't another soul around. It was just her and me. Well, she rings up my stuff and tells me the total comes to four dollars and sixty-five cents. I hand her a five-dollar bill, and just like you said, Frank, I stared right at her. I stared right into her eyes, and she stared at me. We were definitely making eye contact, all right."

"Well, what happened after that?"

"I told her to keep the change. Kind of like a tip, you know? She bagged up my stuff, and I left, but something happened in there, Frank. I really think that woman wants me now."

"George, Clara Butts has been known to do it with farm animals."

"Hey, what she does in the privacy of her own barn is her business."

"Jesus, George, you need professional help," said Frank. Just then, a young woman walked over and set a plate of food in front of Frank. Silence fell on the group of men as they stared at the one end table.

"Good morning, Pepper."

"Good morning, Frank. I hope you enjoy your breakfast."

"If you had anything to do with it, I'm sure that I will."

"See you later, Handsome," she cooed and walked away.

George turned to watch the woman until she disappeared into the back room. "My God, Frank, not while I'm eating," he said. "I almost hurled listening to that conversation."

"You're just jealous, my friend."

"You might be right," he replied. "When an old goat like you gets a young thing like her, I know I must be doing something wrong."

"You just work on your eye contact, and you'll do all right."

For the next several moments, the two men sat quietly and drank their coffee.

"Tell me, Frank," said George. "Did you get any yet?"

"I can't tell you that!"

"Why?"

"Because it's not right!"

"What's not right about it?"

"George, people don't go around telling other people about their sex lives."

"Didn't get any, did ya?"

"I didn't say that."

"Then, you did?"

"I didn't say that either."

Silence fell on that part of the table. "You couldn't handle her, anyhow," said George. "She's too much of a woman for you."

"Oh, and you're now an expert on women. You get Clara Butts to look at you, and you're an expert?"

"Hey, I've had more than my share of women over the years."

"George, you've never been married, and, other than farm animals, you've probably never had sex in your life."

"Not so fast there, my friend. It was only last year that I had a date with a woman."

"Who was it?"

"Hey, never you mind who it was. The important thing is that I've been in the company of a woman."

"Who was it, George?"

"Helen Thompson."

"Helen Thompson? Helen Thompson is eighty-three years old, and I remember that she needed a ride to the doctor's office for a checkup and you took her. Hardly what you would call a date, George."

"Well, we all can't be a Romeo like you, Frank."

"What's the matter with Willard?" asked Frank looking out the window. "He's practically running across the street."

The front door swung wide, and Willard marched across the room towards the end of the table.

"Frank, I was all wrong about that egg farm coming to town," he said pulling up a chair.

"Why the sudden change of heart?" asked Frank sipping his coffee.

Willard leaned back in his chair. "I just think it would be good for the town. You know, jobs and everything."

"Sounds to me like you've figured some angle to make a buck from these people."

"You know that's just like you, Frank. I happen to be a liberal and progressive thinker, and just because you're thinking is still in the dark ages, you make wild accusations of me."

"You stand to make some money if they come to town, don't you?"

"Well, maybe a little, but don't forget that these people are bringing money to this little town. It means jobs, tax money, and, I hear, that they donate money to the town to do with as they see fit."

"I thought you were the one who was afraid of these people. You were certain that there was something sinister going on here."

"Who am I to stand in the way of progress?"

Frank glanced at the other end of the table. "Ben, did you get a chance to talk to your brother about the egg farm?" shouted Frank.

The table of men grew quiet as they looked in Ben's direction. "I talked with Otis over the weekend, and he seems to think that they know what they're doing," said Ben. "They have millions of chickens out there, but everything is under control."

"What about all that manure?" asked Frank.

"Hell, they even have that all figured out. They sell it to the farmers in the area to fertilize their fields."

Frank set his coffee cup on the table. "So, what you're telling me is that there aren't any problems with having millions of chickens confined to a few hundred acres. Is that right?"

"Otis said that there seem to be a lot of flies in the area, but this information is coming from a guy who needs help tying his shoes."

"I don't know," muttered Frank aloud. "It just seems like they're messing with nature."

"Look at it this way, Frank," said Willard moving his chair even closer. "They need to feed all those chickens. Right?" Frank said nothing. "From what I hear, they give top dollar to the local farmers for corn to feed them."

"Oh, so that's your new interest in these people. You plan on making a killing by selling your crops to them."

"Frank, you make it sound like a bad thing. Making a buck is the American way, Frank. It's what it's all about. God bless America."

"Hey, Ben!" shouted Frank. "Does this mean that you're going to sell?"

"Already signed the paperwork," came his answer.

Willard grabbed Frank by the arm. "So, what do you think? Are you going to sign?"

"Has anyone talked to Merle Henson? asked Frank. "I just wonder what he plans to do."

"Who knows anything about Merle Henson? He pretty much keeps to himself."

"Maybe, I'll run out there to see him this afternoon," said Frank," reaching for his wallet. "It wouldn't hurt to see how he's doing anyhow."

"Put that wallet back in your pocket," came a voice from behind. Frank turned around to see Pepper standing over him. The table of men became quiet. "This meal is on me," she continued and lightly kissed the seated man on the top of the head.

The group of men seemed to be frozen as they stared at their friend. Someone uttered a soft, "Wow!" to no one's surprise.

"Well, thank you, young lady," said Frank getting to his feet.

"You beat all, Frank," said George.

"When you got it, you got it," he said and walked out the door.

€ € €

It was early afternoon when Frank closed the back door behind him. He started down the walk towards the garage. The forecast called for rain, and already dark clouds were being ushered in by westerly winds. Frank had been thinking about the egg farm and decided to talk with Merle Henson.

As he turned the corner that led to the garage, Frank heard a noise from inside the barn. He turned and entered through the open doorway stopping just inside the venerable old building.

His eyes quickly scanned the interior. He could find nothing that might have caused the noise until he noticed a swallow who was flapping her wings and jumping from beam to beam in the dusty old rafters of the sagging old barn. She seemed to be upset about something. A barn owl sat in his stately perch several yards away undisturbed by the commotion.

Frank glanced down at the area just below the swallow and noticed a round, gray object. He walked closer to find that it was a nest lying on the ground. Somehow, this carefully made; intricately designed nest had come dislodged from its home in the safety of the rafters of this seldom-used building.

As Frank neared the fallen home, the mother swallow became increasingly agitated. She was now flying frantically in small circles landing on a beam for only a second and then would resume her desperate flight.

Frank stopped only feet from the nest. He could see that it was lying on its side, and two small speckled eggs were lying only inches away on the straw-covered ground. Both appeared to be still intact and had, indeed, survived the fall.

The mother swallow was now screeching in protest to the invader who was standing much too close to her fallen family. The majestic, old owl opened his sleepy eyes to see what was creating this raucous noise in this, otherwise, peaceful dwelling.

Frank stepped back to calm her fears. He knew that there was nothing he could do, and that any intervention from him would prove fatal. He retreated until he was standing in the dark shadows of one corner of the barn. The bird was quiet now. He could see her nervously standing on one of the high beams and then suddenly swoop down to the ground. He was not in a position where he could see her but decided to remain there quietly so as not to disturb her anymore.

Frank studied the old building. Missing shingles from the roof allowed daylight to pour in and spotlight small patches of straw-covered ground throughout the barn. A few boards were missing on the backside of the building allowing even more light to penetrate the dusty interior. Several of the support beams sagged with the weight of all the years gone by.

Frank glared out the dust covered, nearly opaque window. He remembered when the barn was new. It was a simpler time all those years ago. His young children screamed as one chased the other in circles around the feed storage bin in the center of the barn. Cattle, that had been grazing in the north pasture all day, leisurely stroll through the back door of the barn somehow knowing that it was the time of day that feed was being poured into troughs.

Frank breathed deeply. A barrage of smells and odors seemed to linger in his memory. Freshly cut hay and recently ground feed seemed to fill the air. Even the acrid and sometimes foul odors from the livestock seemed to now be a pleasant memory.

It was a warm summer day all those years ago. Frank had just finished milking the cows and was about to feed the chickens when someone grabbed him from behind and screamed his name. His whole body jumped as a reaction and part of the milk that he was carrying spilled over the edges of the buckets.

Frank whirled around to find his wife, Ida, standing before him laughing hysterically. It seemed so strange at the time to see this woman who abhorred practical jokes standing there with her arms still outstretched. Suddenly, she turned and ran. Frank dropped the two buckets of milk to the ground and gave pursuit. Still laughing loudly, she led him in a path that encircled the feed bin in the center of the barn.

The young woman had nearly run completely around the bin when Frank caught her and pulled her to the ground. The two people embraced and rolled over several times in the fresh straw.

"I love you, Mr. Watson," she said with a smile.

"I love you too, Mrs. Watson, and you made me spill milk with that little stunt of yours."

"Try not to be so jumpy, Farmer Frank," she said and rolled over on her back. They both stared up at the rafters of the barn while they caught their breath. "God, I love this barn," she said. "I feel so safe and comfortable when I'm in here. It's like no other place on earth. Do you understand what I mean, Frank?"

"I suppose so," he muttered.

"No, you don't," she said. "You don't understand. You look at this place as storage for hay and a place to milk cows. To me, it's a special place. It's a sanctuary from the world."

"Whatever you say, Ida."

"Frank, I want you to promise me something. I want you to promise me that if I should die before you that you will bury me in this barn. I want to spend an eternity in here."

"I'm not burying you in a barn," he replied. "Besides, there's no way that I'll outlast you anyway."

A gust of wind sent a whirlwind dancing across the floor of the barn. Frank ran his hands through his hair and started for the open doorway. Suddenly, he felt a coldness seem to penetrate his body. He shuddered profusely. It was unlike anything he had ever experienced. For a moment, he could not move, and he found himself dropping to his knees, his arms frozen at his sides.

As quickly as it came, the coldness seemed to escape wildly from his body. The wind ceased, and a stillness fell on the barn and the surrounding area. Suddenly, a warmth poured over his body like sunshine in July. The warmness seemed to spread throughout his body and penetrate his very soul. His body gave a sudden jerk, and his arms slowly raised until they were straight out from his body. His eyes were closed, and his head tilted to one side.

"You're here, aren't you?" asked Frank his arms slowly lowering to his sides. "I can feel you once again." Frank inhaled deeply filling his lungs and then slowly exhaled. "I can smell you. I know you're here." Frank opened his eyes and searched the barn. "I wish you could show yourself. I miss you so much. It's not fair, you know. It's not fair for you to leave me behind like that. I'm lost without you."

Frank got to his feet and turned slowly searching the barn. "Everyone says that this new woman in my life is right for me. They say I should get on with my life. What do you think, Ida? I wish you could tell me, because I don't think it's right. I still love you, Ida, and it just doesn't seem right. I was faithful to you for over forty years of marriage, and nothing has changed now that you're gone. What do I do, Ida? You must tell me what to do."

Frank bowed his head. The warmth that had spread throughout his body quickly dissipated. He got to his feet and looked around the barn. Everything appeared normal again. The wind had subsided and a gentle rain began to fall. Frank looked at the rafters overhead and could see that even the owl's eyes were once again closed, and he had returned to his daytime slumber.

He started for the doorway when he heard the soft chirping sound of a bird. He turned and slowly walked to the back of the barn. There, next to the fallen nest in the soft straw, was the mother swallow. She had, somehow, fashioned a nest from the loose hay and straw and was nestled over the two eggs that held her future offspring.

Frank stared at the mother bird and marveled at her tenacity and dogged persistence despite the obstacles that life had thrown at her. Her home that she had painstakingly built for her new family had taken a disastrous fall, and yet, she undauntedly improvised and proceeded as if it were all a part of the plan.

"Hey, little lady," he said aloud. "Life goes on no matter what happens, right?"

A smile suddenly appeared across Frank's face. "Oh, my God," he muttered aloud. He quickly glanced around the barn and then turned back to the bird in front of him. "Thanks, and good luck to you, Mother Swallow," he said and walked away.

₭ ₭ ₭

It wasn't a long distance to Merle Henson's farm, but it did take a while to get there. The road seemed to wind endlessly through fields of corn and soybeans. Frank enjoyed the trip. He had always loved driving country roads, and today he was happier than he had been in years.

Frank was still smiling when he turned into the Henson farm. He could see a man bent over an old Ford tractor near the barn. "Merle!" he shouted getting out of his truck. "It's Frank Watson. How are you doing?"

An old man straightened his tired back and turned to greet his visitor. "I'm fine, Frank," he replied thrusting out his hand. "How are you?"

"Doing great," Frank said taking his hand. "Problems with your tractor, Merle?"

"Got a loose wheel, for Christ's sakes. I swear to God if it isn't one thing it's another."

"Need any help while I'm here?"

"No, thanks, Frank. Hopefully, I'll figure out what's wrong before it falls off the tractor. What brings you over to this run-down farm, anyhow?"

"There are some people interested in buying up farmland around here. I just wondered if they've already been here to see you?"

"They sure have, Frank."

"If you don't mind my asking, Merle, but what did you tell them?"

"I sent them packing, Frank. In fact, I told them to get off my land."

"Why did you do that, Merle?"

"I don't really know for sure," he said leaning to one side to spit. "Something just doesn't seem right about it. I can't explain it. I can tell you one thing though. I got into one big fight with the wife when she heard how much they were offering."

"Irma wants to sell the farm?"

"She never was much of a farmer's wife. Got too much of the city in her. She nearly flipped out when she heard I had a chance to sell it.

"Sorry to hear that, Merle."

"Don't worry," he replied. "She'll get over it. She always does. Want to come inside for a cup of coffee, Frank?"

"Wish I could, Merle, but I have too much to do," he replied walking towards his truck. "Jesus, Merle, you need to stop by the house. I swear you haven't been by since the funeral."

"I'll do that, Frank, and, by God, that's a promise."

"See that you do, my friend," said Frank starting his engine.

"Good bye, Frank," said Merle as the truck pulled out of the driveway.

6 POP

Frank spent most of the day on Tuesday preparing a picnic lunch for his invited guest who would be coming the following day. He had bought all the food necessary for a fried chicken and potato salad lunch. Even though it had been years since he had prepared such a meal, he was still determined to give it a try.

Frank got up early on Wednesday morning. The potato salad was already completed, and it was now time to fry the chicken. He dipped the pieces of poultry into flour and dropped them in a black iron skillet. The loud sizzling sound seemed to echo a protest throughout the kitchen. Every few minutes, he would turn the pieces of meat in the skillet until they were a deep golden brown, and by ten o'clock, his picnic lunch was ready.

"Well, I'll be," said Toad walking through the back door. "I think I've seen everything now. Frank Watson in the kitchen."

"You haven't seen anything yet. Now, wait right there," said Frank rushing across the kitchen. He grabbed a cup, filled it with fresh coffee and set it on the table. "Have a seat, my friend, and enjoy a cup of coffee that you don't have to fix."

"My God, Frank, I'm stunned," she said taking a seat at the table. "You've actually been cooking, Frank. By the way, what is that smell?"

"Oh, that?" asked Frank. "That's just some chicken that I fried up. You know me, Toad, always got something on the stove."

"I still can't believe it. This woman must be something special to get you into the kitchen. When is she coming over, Frank?"

"She'll be here at noon."

"Is there anything I can do to help?"

"No, thanks. I'm all set."

"Frank, are you all right with this now? You know, with Ida and everything."

"Yeah, everything is just fine," he answered. "I know now that she's okay with this."

"Frank, are you telling me that it's all right with Ida that you see this woman?"

"That's exactly what I'm saying. I've been given a sign, and I know it was from her."

"What kind of sign, Frank?"

"It was something as simple as a mother bird and her two eggs. I know it sounds crazy, but it was as much a sign as that shoe brush on the night stand.

"Well, I think it's wonderful, Frank," said Toad getting to her feet. I didn't think I'd ever see you get back into the saddle again.

It's just fantastic. Besides, it might improve your personality somewhat if you were to get laid."

"Toad!" Frank exclaimed as he followed her across the kitchen.

"Hey, you've been a little cranky lately, but right now, I'm going to get out of your way," she said opening the back door. "It would hardly do to have a woman leaving your house when she arrives."

"Good point! You're right! Now, get out of here!" said Frank closing the door after her.

"Good luck!" she shouted as she hurried away.

It was just after noon when Frank heard a knock on the front door. He ran his hand through his thinning hair and started for the door.

"Well, hello there," said Frank swinging the door wide.

"Hi, Frank," said Pepper stepping inside. "My, what a nice place you have here and so neat."

"Surprised?"

"Quite frankly, yes I am. I don't know. I guess I expected to see something less than neat without a woman."

"So, basically, you're saying that men are slobs."

"I wouldn't have chosen that particular word, but it does seem to work."

"How do you feel about picnics?" asked Frank walking into the kitchen.

"I love picnics, but not on a day like this."

"What are you talking about?"

"You haven't looked outside lately, have you?"

Frank walked over to the window. Dark, ominous clouds hung low in the sky, and a gentle rain was falling. "Just my luck," said Frank. "I had everything fixed, packed and ready to go. I even had a checkered tablecloth. No picnic is complete without one."

"You don't suppose that checkered tablecloth would spread out on this kitchen table, do you?" asked Pepper with a smile.

Frank looked down at the table and back at Pepper. "Do you mean an indoor picnic?"

"Why not?"

"I had a spot picked out over at Henson Creek under an Elm tree that is so big and so old, it was probably planted by Moses, himself."

"There are no ants at an indoor picnic."

Frank studied the picnic basket and then smiled. "Let's do it," he said and began to unload the contents. Within minutes, they were sitting down to eat on a checkered tablecloth.

"Why fried chicken?" asked Pepper setting down a half-eaten chicken leg.

"What do you mean?"

"I fixed chicken the other night, and you come right back with your own. As good as this taste, I think you're trying to show me up."

"No, no. Not me. I learned a long time ago never to show up a woman."

"Did you learn that from your wife, Frank?"

"Mostly."

Pepper got up and poured two cups of coffee. "Frank, everyone in town tells me how much you loved your wife, Ida," she said sitting back down. "Tell me, Frank, what was she like?"

"What was she like?" I don't know. It's hard to explain. I think the best way to describe her is to tell you about lunch time."

"Lunch time, Frank? It figures that a man would describe a woman in terms of food."

Frank was oblivious to what she was saying. He turned and stared out the window, taking a sip from his coffee cup and returning it to the table. "No matter what field I was plowing or fence I was mending, I always knew when that wonderful, old woman had lunch ready. I could walk through that door, and she would be setting the last bowl of food on the table."

"Well, Frank, I'm sure that after all those years, you probably just got into the habit of coming home at the same time."

"Didn't have a watch; never owned one. We just knew. I can't explain it, but she knew when I'd be home, and I knew when lunch was ready. I know it sounds crazy, but we really could read each other's mind. I always knew what she was going to say before she opened her mouth and knew what she wanted even before she asked. We thought, felt, and functioned as one. I was the part who worked the farm, and she was the part who took care of the house. Different parts doing different things but all a part of the same person. Throughout time there have been couples meant for each other. There have been songs written about it and movies made about it, but no two people were meant for each other like Ida and me."

Pepper set down her fork and leaned back in her chair. "Sounds like a very special woman, Mr. Watson. Sounds like a tough act to follow."

I won't deny it," he said. "She was truly a wonderful woman."

Pepper took a sip from her coffee cup and set it back down. "Frank, you're a tough and hardworking man, and yet it's obvious to everyone who knows you that you're a kind and sensitive man. Why is that, Frank? How did you turn out the way you did?"

"Oh, I don't know. I'm not even sure that I turned out all that great."

"Don't be so modest, Frank Watson. Tell me, what were your parents like?"

"My dad is in a nursing home," said Frank. "My mother has been gone for quite some time."

"What was she like?"

"What was my mother like?" asked Frank getting to his feet. "The best way to answer that is for you read a letter that she wrote to me when I was a young man." He walked over to a desk and opened one of the drawers. He removed a yellowed stack of papers and returned to his seat. "I remember the day she handed this letter to me. It was my twenty-first birthday, and I was soon to be married. It was a bright sunny day in June, and I had the whole world ahead of me. It was probably the finest birthday present anyone ever gave me, and I've saved it all these years."

Frank handed the old and fragile letter to Pepper, and she began to read: Today, you are 21! Happy birthday, Son! In just a week, the girl who is now first in your life and heart will become your bride. To both of you, may God be kind and grant you the joy of a very happily married life.

There is a special ache in your father's and my heart in relinquishing you, the youngest of our three sons. We would be lying if we did not say this was so. Please, don't misunderstand us. We know this is the plan of life; to seek, love, and marry. Then, to fulfill this marriage, a family. Our wish is that your children may bring you the delight and joy you have given us.

In the past month, the irritations of various problems have made you a bit edgy. In fact, your attitude towards me is an echo of you when you were about the age of six. If it was my duty to discipline you or deny you a privilege, you would stamp your foot, blaze a danger signal from your eyes as you announced to one and all that this world would be better off if there weren't any women. When you reached 15 or 16, you reconsidered this statement and made qualifications!

It's my guess that all true mothers cherish within their memories bits of each one of their children's progress from cradle to altar. There is one that I would like to share with you, and I hope that someday you may have one as precious. For precious they are. Memories can be rare jewels, which neither thief can steal nor rust corrupt.

It was the Saturday afternoon before Easter Sunday, and I would guess you were about nine years old. We were expecting company for Easter Sunday dinner. Some of the house cleaning remained, and I had a start-from-scratch cake started. It was the first balmy spring day after a cold, miserable winter. You spent the morning digging worms to go fishing, and you had your poles, bobbers, sinkers, and hooks in top condition. The problem? There was no one to go fishing with you. Your older brothers had disappeared, and the buddies of your age had gone to Grandma's and other places. The busy neighborhood seemed deserted. You sat on a kitchen chair with a look of desolation. You were too young to go alone, and had no one to go with you.

Finally, in desperation, you asked, "Mom, will you go fishing with me?" I held my hand on the mixer after stopping it. Never would I be ready for tomorrow if I didn't keep plugging away. Who knows though? Maybe, tomorrow would never come. The chance of your asking me to go fishing with you again, without a doubt, would never happen again. This was a case of pure desperation on your part.

We gathered up fishing tackle and were on our way in five minutes. Cake was still in the process of "scratch."

It was the most beautiful and reverent three hours of my life. The pure enjoyment of the beautiful day and the sharing of your experience of the first fishing of the year made an almost bittersweet pleasure because I knew that it would probably never happen again. We talked of many things and shared the wonders of the day. A school of fish played close to the bank. Now and then, a turtle would surface, look us over, and retire to the comfortable depths from which he had emerged. A weeping willow was overhead, and it seemed that we spent most of the afternoon untangling your fishing line from it. We even joked about fishing more in the tree than in the river. When we started for home, our catch of fish was small, but the catch of treasures in my heart was like gold. It was a jewel perfect day.

Now, son, it is my hope that someday you may have such an experience. Maybe, instead of a son, you might have a lovely, dark-haired, dark-eyed daughter, and her date has stood her up. Where else to go for comfort and understanding but father. You may never be asked again. So, please son; do not be too busy to share yourself with one so close to your heart.

Finally, something bothers me. Remember your high school graduation day? Never are the stars so bright or the horizons so wide as they are on this day. While speaking to your class, your school superintendent remarked that what you are is God's gift to you, and what you become is your gift to God.

On the way home with your father and me, you were quiet and thoughtful. Out of the silence, you wondered aloud about what you could do in life to serve God. How would seeking a career to make money be considered an act of serving God. I replied that it is the way of things. You earn money to sustain a family, and so on it goes.

You didn't seem satisfied with the answer. This is good. There is promise for growth in your life. Are you still thinking about it? Is something still there waiting to be answered?

Happy Birthday, Son,
Mom

Pepper brushed the tears from her eyes and laid the letter on the table in front of Frank. "I guess I know now what your mother was like, and I know how you became so sensitive," she said softly. "She must have been quite a woman."

Frank got to his feet and walked across the kitchen. He leaned over the sink and gazed out the window. "She died a short time after writing that letter," he said with an unsteady voice.

Pepper walked over to Frank and gently laid her hand on his forearm. He wiped his eyes with his handkerchief and slowly turned around. Still hanging onto his arm, she gazed into his eyes.

Frank placed his hands on her shoulders, both shaking nervously. He stared into her teary, blue eyes. Her lips were slightly parted. Neither one spoke as he leaned over, his lips nearing hers. She lurched upwards slightly as she stood on her toes. His face was now level with hers. He could feel her sweet breath on his skin. He closed his eyes, and she, hers.

Suddenly, the stillness was assaulted by the offensive ringing of the telephone. Frank snapped his head back as if awakening from a dream. He glanced at the phone and then back at the woman standing in front of him. Neither one spoke as he walked over to answer the phone.

"Frank Watson?"

"Yes."

"This is the nursing home calling. We seem to have a problem with your father and would like for you to come down here. Is that possible?"

He turned and looked at Pepper for a moment and then turned back around. "I'll be there in a few minutes," he said and hung up the phone.

"Is there something wrong, Frank?" she asked.

"Something's wrong with Pop," he said. "I need to run over to the nursing home. Would you like to come along?"

"Sure! I'd love to!"

"Don't be so enthusiastic. You haven't seen this place yet," he said starting for the door.

"Pretty bad?" she asked. Frank just stared at her and said nothing.

It was a short trip to the nursing home, and within minutes, they were pulling into the parking lot. They both got out of the truck and walked through the front door.

"Mr. Watson," came a voice from behind them. Frank spun around to see the Assistant Director walking towards him. "Mr. Watson, I'm sorry to bother you, but, as you know, we do have a policy to contact members of the family if anything unusual should happen."

"That's quite all right," said Frank. "What did he do this time?"

"Your father seems a bit agitated today, Mr. Watson. Even medication doesn't seem to help. He's been screaming obscenities at people and has even hit one of the other patients."

"He hit someone? Did he hurt him?"

"Fortunately, no. The blow missed the man's face and hit him on the shoulder."

"Do you have any idea why he did such a thing?"

"When your father is in his wheelchair, he has a favorite place in the hallway that he likes. There's a spot near the drinking fountain that he considers to be his own territory. This morning, your father found another patient in his spot, and he hit him."

"My God, I'm so sorry," said Frank. "I'll go talk with him to see if I can find out what's bothering him."

"Mr. Watson, there is one more problem."

"What's that?"

"Your father's talking suicide again." Frank said nothing as he stared down the hallway. "Just thought you should know."

"Thanks," said Frank and started walking in the direction of his father's room. Moments later, they were standing in front of Ned Watson's room.

"You wait here while I talk with him," said Frank turning to Pepper.

"You're not going to leave me out here by myself, are you?" she asked. "What if one of these people come after me?"

"Don't worry," said Frank. "For the most part, they are all harmless. However, if any of them tries to bother you, tell him you're from the planet, Argo, and you'll vaporize the whole place if he doesn't leave you alone."

"Are you kidding?"

"No, I'm telling you it works every time," he said as he walked in the room and closed the door behind him.

"How are you doing, Pop?" asked Frank as he leaned over and kissed the old man on the forehead.

"No goddamn good," he snapped. Frank stepped back and stared at his father. Over the years since he had entered the home, he had seen his father exhibit many different moods. He's been angry, and he's been depressed. He has seen him when he remembers every detail about the past, and then other times, he doesn't even recognize his own son.

Today was different. He had never seen his father like this. His face had a troubled, yet pitiful look that seemed to be begging for mercy. Frank felt an aching inside. Something was deeply wrong with his father. He could see that, but he wasn't sure what was causing the old man such distress. "Is your butt hurting you, Dad?"

"Yes," he said shifting from side to side.

"Do you want me to have them put something on it?"

"Who are you, anyhow?"

"I'm your son, Dad. It's me, Frank."

"If you're my son, then get me out of here!"

"You can't leave, Dad. You have to stay here."

Ned stopped thrashing and stared into Frank's eyes. His face had an angry look about it. "Get me the hell out of here!" he shouted. "I can't stand it in here anymore!"

It was painful for Frank to see his father like this. Here was this strong and courageous man who was the head of the family, who worked hard all his life, and was now sitting in a diaper that needed to be changed. Frank loved his father and respected him all his life, but there was no doubt that the best thing was for him to simply pass away. Everyone who knew Ned Watson agreed that if he were capable of making decisions, he would not want to continue living like this.

"Frank," said his father, "Bend over here. I need to tell you something." Fear raced through his body as he leaned over the bed. "Frank, I can't take it anymore. I want to die."

"Don't talk like that, Dad."

Ned grabbed his son by both arms. "You must help me, son. I want to die."

Frank stared into the eyes of this wonderful, old man whom he had called his father for all his life and saw something he had never seen. He saw fear on the face of a man who was ready to die but was unsure of his own destiny. From the agony of the uncertainty of his fate, he was begging for guidance and direction.

Suddenly, Frank felt the burden of responsibility shift from his father's shoulders to his own. All his life, Frank had looked to his father for help and advice, and suddenly, his father was staring at him with eyes that were pleading for help. Ned Watson was ready to die, and it was Frank's duty to make the right decision to guide his actions.

"I can't, Dad," said Frank taking his hand. "I can't do anything that would help you end your life. God considers it a sin to take a life, even your own."

"God!" shouted Ned. "Don't talk to me about God! No God would allow someone to live like this! If God were merciful, he'd have taken me a long time ago. No, sir. It's a goddamn shame that anyone should have to live like this! Hell, we treat animals better than we treat humans. If a dog or a horse is in pain or can't function because he's too old, we put him out of his misery. Then, we tell everyone how humane we are. Now, I know I don't think so good any more, but what about me? Why can't I get the same mercy that a dog would receive?"

Frank moved his chair closer to the bed and leaned over until he was only inches from his father's face. "Dad, do you remember when I was a little kid, and you bought me a BB gun? Do you remember that, Pop?"

The old man stopped his fidgeting "Sure, I remember," he said.

"God, I loved that gun," said Frank. "I was only about eight or nine years old as I recall and thought I was the toughest guy in the world now that I was the proud owner of a BB gun.

I remember that it was only a couple days after you gave me that gun that I was behind the house shooting at just about anything in sight. I didn't know it at the time but you were watching me from a window when, suddenly, I began shooting at the birds sitting high up in the trees. I don't know whether I believed that I could hit one of them. They seemed so far off. Maybe, I thought of them as inanimate object. I don't know. All I know is that it wasn't long before I scored a direct hit, and to my surprise a bird began its descent from its perch, falling gracelessly as it bounced from one limb to another. I must say I was surprised. I never really thought that I would shoot one.

I remember that I walked over to the bird with a certain amount of apprehension. I wasn't sure if I should strut like some big game hunter after the kill, or cautiously creep up to the innocent little animal that I had needlessly destroyed.

I knelt beside the fallen bird, and with the end of my gun, I gently turned it over. From its pale red underside, I knew that it was a female robin. I remember wishing that it was only stunned, and that it would suddenly awaken and fly away, but that was not to be. Her head dangled, lifelessly, to one side, and a small trickle of blood oozed from under her feathers and dripped onto the ground.

I nudged the bird with my gun hoping to arouse it from some deep sleep. Nothing. By now, the tears were flowing from my eyes as I finally came to realize what I had done. A sweet and innocent life had been taken, and it was my fault.

I don't know how long you had been standing beside me, but, suddenly, you were there bending down on one knee. You stayed there for the longest time. I remember that. I was dying inside. I felt so bad. I had done something very bad and deserved to be punished, and you calmly stared at the dead bird.

Finally, you turned to me and asked me if I understood what had happened here. I muttered something about an accident and how I'd never do it again and then you told me something that I never forgot. In fact, I'm sure that was your intention that it would be a day that I would remember all my life. You told me that today was the day that the life of a small bird ended. Hardly seems significant in the big scheme of things, but nonetheless, we have one less bird in the world today. Tomorrow, there will be one less song being sung by a creature whose only goal in life is to give happiness.

You, then, laid a hand on my shoulder, and when I finally worked up the nerve to look you in the eye, I noticed a tear falling down your cheek. To this day, I can't remember another time that I ever saw you cry. You told me that since God loves all life, even the lowly robin, and there must be a reason for this seemingly senseless death. It was then that you told me something that would guide my life from then on. You told me that, without doubt, God sacrificed that little bird so that I would learn a valuable lesson. I would be a better person after having seen how precious life is. Life must be preserved at all cost. Then, you told me that I should always remember the lesson that I learned so that the robin's dying would not be in vain. Do you remember that, Dad?"

Ned was relaxed now. He was smiling as he stared out the window lost in rich memories of the past. He turned to face his son, his eyes twinkled. "You never shot any more birds, did you?"

Frank laughed. "I don't think I ever shot that BB gun again."

"I didn't expect you to turn into a sissy."

"Well, I knew I wouldn't be shooting any more birds. I couldn't stand the guilt."

"That's because you're a sissy," he said. Both men became quiet. They stared at each other, smiling with the knowledge that they had shared a memory and were now sharing a moment, a moment of peace and serenity that they had not known in years. Ned took his son's hand and buried it within the safety of his own. "I love you, son," he said with a smile.

"I love you too, Dad."

Frank brushed the tears from his eyes. "Oh, my God!" he shouted. "I completely forgot! I brought someone to see you. She's waiting in the hallway."

"She? You brought a woman to see me? Who is it?"

"She's a friend of mine, and I want you to meet her," Frank said starting for the door.

"Is everything all right?" asked Frank as he opened the door.

Pepper quickly stepped inside the room. "Do you know there's a guy out there in his underwear who thinks he's Superman?"

"Did he give you the once over?"

"Yes, as a matter of fact, he did."

"There are those who swear he can see through clothes." Pepper glanced down at her body for a moment and then back to Frank.

"Pop, I want you to meet Pepper. Pepper, this is my father, Ned Watson."

"Glad to meet you, Mr. Watson."

"Don't you have any self-respect?" asked Ned pulling up his blanket.

"Sir?"

"Hanging around with the likes of this fellow," said Ned pointing at his son. "You couldn't have much self respect."

"Oh, I don't know," she said. "He's not so bad."

"Well, I can see he's got you brainwashed," said the old man. "You're wasting your time, anyway."

"Why is that, sir?"

"Because he's got such a little penis!" he shouted.

"Dad!"

"Won't do you much good, being so tiny and all. Really isn't his fault. Small dicks run through the family. They say that when my grandpa used to urinate, he would sometimes grab a hair by mistake and piss his pants."

"Jesus, Dad, will you behave?"

"I'm no different, you know. Sorry, to say. Didn't bother me much, but it sure did frustrate Frank's mother."

"And this is his good mood," said Frank. "Okay, Pop, I think you've humiliated me enough, not to mention the embarrassment you've caused my friend."

"Unless I miss my guess, I don't think you've got much to worry about. I'd say she can take it and dish it out as well."

"I grew up with two older brothers," she announced.

"See there! She hasn't learned anything new here today."

"Well, I can tell you feel better, Dad," said Frank. "Is there anything I can get you?"

"The only thing I want is the hell out of here, and you won't help me with that."

"Well, here it comes, Dad. It's time to ask you the question."

"What question?"

"The same damn question I've been asking you for the last two years. What did you get me on my sixteenth birthday?"

Ned paused and turned to Pepper. "Hey, young lady, come over here." She came closer and leaned over the bed. "Do me a favor, will you? Find out what in the hell I gave this guy for his sixteenth birthday. He's driving me nuts about that goddamn birthday present. Personally, I think he has forgotten, and that's why he keeps asking me."

"If I find out anything, I'll let you know."

"All right, Dad, we have to be going. You behave yourself, all right?"

"Yeah, yeah, yeah."

"I mean it, Dad. You can't go hitting people just because they're sitting in your spot."

"That might be so, but I'll bet that when you walk down that hallway, you won't see old man Fogerty near the drinking fountain."

"You're impossible, Dad," said Frank starting for the door. "Got to go."

"Young lady!" shouted Ned. "Come here a minute. I want to see you alone." Frank paused and stared at his father. "Go on and get out of here. I want to talk to her in private."

"I'll be right outside," said Frank and closed the door behind him.

Ned turned to Pepper and said, "Give me your hand." She extended it in his direction, and he smothered it with both of his. "I've been around a long time, and I'm a pretty fair judge of character. The one thing that I'm sure about is that you're the one for my son."

"Well, thank you, Mr. Watson. I really think..."

Ned squeezed her hand tightly and raised his head from his pillow. "Make him forget!" he said with a stern and commanding voice. Pepper said nothing as she stared at the man. "Make him forget all about the past and give him a reason to dream about the future."

"I'll do my best."

"You've got to do better than that. If you two are going to have any kind of happiness, you have to make him forget the past."

Pepper smiled and said, "I will do my best, Mr. Watson. I promise you."

"Good. Now, get along with you," he said with a wave of his hand. "We can't leave him out there too long. He's scares too easily."

"I'll see you again, real soon," she said with a smile as she backed away from him. Ned winked at her as she turned and walked out of the room.

Frank was quiet on the way back to the house. In fact, he didn't even ask what his father had said to her in private. Within minutes, they were pulling into Frank's driveway and walking up to the back door.

Frank took a seat at the kitchen table, and Pepper pulled up a chair beside him. "Are you all right?" she asked.

"Yeah. Just thinking about my dad."

Frank got to his feet and walked across the kitchen. He leaned against the counter and gazed outside. "He's just an average man to most people. In fact, when he dies, he will leave behind nothing that's noteworthy. He'll leave no great works of art nor published novels, no sculptures or musical compositions. There's a real good chance that within a very short time after he's gone, there will be no one who will even remember him, but to me, he's the greatest man I've ever known. He was, is, and always will be my hero.

Pepper stood and walked across the kitchen. She grabbed his arm and gently tugged on it. Frank slowly turned around until he was staring into her eyes. He leaned over until his head was level with hers and gently pressed his lips against hers.

7 THE EGG FARM

The next morning began as so many other spring mornings with life-giving sunshine nourishing the earth below. Frank swung around in bed and placed his bare feet on the cool floor. The tops of his pajamas were missing so he slipped on the bottoms and walked across the bedroom floor. He walked through the living room and into the kitchen. It was there that he found the solution to the mystery of the missing pajama top.

"Good morning," said Frank standing in the doorway.

"Good morning, Frank," said Pepper turning a pancake in the skillet. "Hope you didn't mind my borrowing your PJ top."

"Any time," said Frank. "They look much better on you than they could ever look on me.

"I found two boxes of pancake mix in the pantry, so I kind of figured you don't eat eggs every morning."

"Pancakes are fine," he said. "My God, what time is it?"

"It's nearly ten o'clock."

"Aren't you late for work?"

"I work the late shift today. Don't go in until noon."

"I haven't slept this late in years. Must have been something that happened to me last night," he said with a grin. "I've had this smile on my face all morning, and I can't seem to get rid of it." He leaned over and lightly kissed her on the cheek.

Pepper scooped the pancake from the skillet and dropped it on a plate. "Thank you, Mr. Watson, for last night," she said. "I am, truly, a new woman this morning." She quickly kissed him on the lips and handed him the plate of food.

She turned to pour two cups of coffee when, suddenly, the back door opened and in stepped Toad. She stopped at the entrance to the kitchen and stared at Frank holding a plate of food and wearing only his red and black checkered pajama bottoms. She, then, glanced at the young woman wearing the matching top. At that moment, she was leaning over the counter reaching for the coffeepot with her rear partially exposed. Both Frank and Pepper looked at each other and then at Toad.

Several moments passed. No one said anything. No one even moved.

Finally, Toad started walking across the kitchen. "Well, I don't know who you are, but I'm glad you're here. This is one of the few times that I have ever come over here and coffee was already made."

Toad leaned over to take the coffeepot. "Now, why don't you let me pour the coffee. You must be feeling a draft. Your tail feathers are showing."

Pepper jumped and covered herself with both hands. "You must be Toad," she said whipping one of her hands around and extending it in her direction. "I'm Pepper."

"I'm Toad," she said taking her hand, "and I'll shake your hand even if I know where it's been."

"Sorry," said Pepper pulling her hand away.

"Oh, that's all right. Don't worry about me. I live on a farm," she said as she finished pouring coffee.

Pepper glared at her with a puzzled look.

"They tell me you're from the big city. Is that right?" she asked as she took a seat at the table.

"Yes, that's right."

"Well, we're glad you moved here, but I have to believe that it's going to take some time to adjust to a small town like ours."

"No, I don't think..."

"Just remember that everything you heard about small town life is true. There is no such thing as privacy. Everyone knows everything about everybody. Hell, I knew that you two were going to shack up last night before Frank did.

Pepper eased herself into a chair next to Frank. "My goodness, that's amazing."

"Amazing?" asked Toad. "You ain't seen nothing yet. I swear I know when someone gets pregnant around here before he tells her to sit still while he gets a towel. Just remember, Honey, there are three forms of communication in a small town; telegraph, telephone, and tell a woman."

"Well, I hear a lot of things at the restaurant, but I never know what's true or not."

"It doesn't matter if it's true or not. Hell, that's the least of any concern. All that matters is that it's really juicy. If you ever want to know if something's true or not, just call me. I can sort out the good stuff from the bad, and I'm on call twenty-four hours a day."

"You know, Toad, you really need to find something to do with your life," said Frank. "What you're doing isn't healthy."

"Speaking of health, did you hear what happened to Merle Hensen?"

"No, Toad, tell me. What happened to Merle Hensen."

"Well, he doesn't have to worry about his prostate anymore, because he's dead."

"He's what?"

"Merle Hensen is dead."

"Oh, my God," said Frank. "What happened?"

"Farming accident from what I hear," said Toad. "They say he was plowing in one of his fields, and one of his wheels came off. He didn't have a chance. I guess the tractor rolled over on top of him and crushed him like a bug."

Frank became silent. He got to his feet and walked over to the kitchen window.

Toad glanced at Pepper and then back to Frank. "Are you all right, Frank?"

He turned slowly around and leaned against the counter. "It just seems so strange," he muttered.

"What seems so strange, Frank?" asked Toad.

"I was out to see Merle just the other day, and he was in the middle of fixing that wheel."

"Must have done a poor job of it," said Toad getting to her feet.

"I don't think so," he muttered with a blank stare. "I don't think so."

"Well, I'm going to leave you kids alone," said Toad starting for the door. "Nice meeting you, Pepper."

"Nice meeting you," she said.

Frank remained quiet and was still leaning against the counter after Toad left.

"Is everything all right?" asked Pepper.

"I need to take you home as soon as you get dressed. I have something to do."

"What's wrong, Frank? You seem upset about something."

"I need to stop at the Hensen farm. I just want to look at that tractor. You don't mind, do you?"

"Not at all. In fact, I'll be ready in just a few minutes."

₭ ₭ ₭

It was just after noon when Frank pulled into the Hensen's driveway. He parked his truck and walked to the back door. The farm was quiet and appeared to be deserted. He knocked three times and stepped back from the door. There was no answer. He, then, walked over to the garage and peered in the window. Since the family car was gone, he assumed Irma had gone to town quite possibly to make funeral arrangements.

Frank walked over to the barn and opened the door. There, just inside the door, was the ill-fated tractor. One of the wheels was missing leaving one side of the tractor supported by a jack. Frank scanned the interior of the barn until his eyes fell onto the missing wheel. It was leaning against a wall in a remote corner of the barn.

Frank walked across the barn and stood in front of the wheel. He knelt and ran his finger across the surface and found that it had not been soiled by any dirt or grease. He tried again at another spot and found nothing.

It was then that Frank heard a car door closing. He stood and walked to the entrance to the barn. As he passed the tractor, he glanced at the other wheel that was still attached. He opened the door and there was Irma slowly walking towards him with her head buried in her hands.

"Irma. It's me, Frank."

"I told him to get someone to fix that wheel," she said drying her eyes. "It was that damn stubbornness that got him killed."

"What happened, Irma?"

"That wheel in the barn, Frank, did you see it?"

"Yes, Irma. I saw it."

"Came off while he was plowing, Frank. I told him to get it fixed right. Damn stubborn man. If he'd done like I said, none of this would have happened."

"Irma, I was out here when he was fixing that wheel. Everything seemed all right at the time."

"Oh, yes. That's right. You were here the same day those other fellows were here."

"What other fellows?"

"A couple men in suits from those egg factories came to see Merle shortly after you left."

"Did Merle say what they wanted?"

"Same thing they always want. They want to buy this farm. Looks like they're finally going to get what they want."

"Why? Do you intend to sell to these people?"

"I don't have any choice," Irma said. "I can't maintain a farm by myself. Besides, I've had enough of farm life. It's just no good for me, Frank. The solitude and the loneliness. It's not good for a body to be like that. I've wanted to move for years, but Merle wouldn't hear of it. Guess it don't matter much now."

"I'm really sorry, Irma. I hope everything works out for you."

"Thanks, Frank," she said.

"If there's anything I can do, please let me know," he said and started for his truck.

⁚ ⁚ ⁚

The next morning brought a warm, sunny start to a bright, spring day. It was the kind of day that farmers dreamed of all winter long. It was a day for plowing. It was a day for sowing seed. It was the kind of day that retired farmers felt the warm wind and yearned to be sitting atop his John Deere in some remote field of rich and fertile soil.

Frank opened the door of the restaurant and let himself in. The air was thick with smoke from the lit cigarettes and pipes. A stillness fell on the table of men as Frank walked to the back of the restaurant to pour himself a cup of coffee.

"Morning, George," said Frank as he took his seat.

"Morning, Frank."

"George, why do I get the feeling that everyone is staring at me?"

"Gee, Frank. I want to be just like you when I grow up."

"What are you talking about?"

"You're the talk of the town, Frank. There is nothing else to talk about. Nobody wants to talk about anything else. No one cares about anything else. It's you, buddy, only you," he said putting his arm around his shoulder.

"George, will you tell me what's going on?"

"Well, the old maids in town are talking about you and some young thing about half your age shacking up."

"Well, that's not so bad."

"That's not the half of it. The rumor is that Toad came over to make it a threesome."

"What?"

"Boy, Frank, when you break out of your slump, you don't mess around."

"Damn busybodies in this town," said Frank with a scowl.

"That's not the worst of it."

"Now, what?"

"Do you see the way these guys are staring at you, Frank," said George pointing at the men sitting at the table.

Frank took quick, furtive glance and turned back to his friend. "So, what's their problem?"

"They're just like everyone else in this town. They want to get a rope and string you up for not wanting to sell your land to the egg people."

Frank took another quick glance at the table of faces staring in his direction. "Are you kidding me? I thought they were upset about something important."

"It is important, Frank. Any time this little town gets a shot at some serious money coming in, it is extremely important."

"Do you mean to tell me that these people think the egg farm will be that big of a deal for Springfield?"

"The Second Coming of the Messiah pales in comparison."

"I've got to give up eggs for breakfast," muttered Frank. "They're giving me indigestion."

"Good morning, Frank," said Pepper carrying a tray of food to the table.

"Good morning, Beautiful," said Frank. "What's a pretty woman like you doing in a place like this?"

"When I was a little girl, I couldn't decide whether I wanted to be an astronaut or an Indian Chief. So, here I am."

"You should have held out for one of the other jobs. I think there's bigger tips involved."

Pepper began setting plates of food in front of the men. When her tray was empty, she returned to the one end of the table.

"The usual, Frank?" she asked.

"No, thanks," he said. "Bring me a stack of pancakes. Eggs don't seem to agree with me, lately."

Pepper glanced at the table of men and leaned over Frank's shoulder. "What's the matter with your little friends? They look like they aren't going to let you play in their sandbox."

"Oh, don't worry about them," said Frank. "They're just having a little snit. That's all."

"I'll be right back with your breakfast."

"All right, Frank," came a voice from one end of the table. A silence fell on the restaurant. "What are you planning to do?"

"Who's asking?" asked Frank turning towards the table of faces.

"It's me, Joe Parker."

"Joe Parker. How's your son doing, Joe. Haven't seen much of him since he ran off with Millie."

"Never mind that shit, Frank. Tell us. We want to know. What are your plans?"

"Well, Joe, I plan to eat a stack of pancakes when they get here, and then I plan to go home and watch my favorite soap opera."

"Jesus, there's no talking to him," said Joe.

"Frank, we need to know if you plan to sell your farm to the egg people," said Willard Miller.

"Well, I have news for all of you. I don't think you're going to like this news, but here goes anyhow. What I do with my farm is none of your business."

"That's where you're wrong, Frank," said Willard. "What you do with your farm is very much our business. It means a lot to this town, Frank. We're talking about a lot of money, the kind of money that could get this town back on its feet."

"It's always money with you, Willard, isn't it?" barked Frank. "The almighty buck! Well, let me tell you something, Willard. That farm means more than life itself to me, and I have no intentions of selling it."

"Jesus, Frank," muttered Willard. "You're as bull-headed as your father."

An ominous silence fell on the room. Everyone seemed to be frozen in place. All eyes turned to Frank as he slowly arose from his seat.

"Willard," said Frank in a low and menacing voice. "Don't you ever talk about my father like that again." He stood there for several moments staring at the man at the other end of the table. No one spoke. No one moved. All eyes turned back to Willard.

"Sorry, Frank," he said softly.

Frank sat down in his chair, and everyone continued eating their breakfast.

Frank turned to George. "Too bad we don't have another restaurant in town," he said. "This place is beginning to stink."

"Don't let them bother you, Frank," said George. "For they know not what they do."

"I know. I know. I shouldn't let them get to me, but someday that Willard is going to get his. Besides, it's all crap anyway. Nobody has even approached me about selling the farm."

A hand came out of nowhere and set a plate of pancakes in front of Frank.

Pepper leaned over and whispered into his ear. "When am I going to see you again?" she asked.

"This Monday is Memorial Day," said Frank. "I was wondering if you could come over for a cookout."

"That sounds like..."

"Be careful. Before you answer, I should warn you. It's traditional that my kids come over to the house for all three of the summer holidays. So, unfortunately, you'll have to meet them."

"You make it sound like they were good friends with Charles Manson or something."

"Sometimes, I wonder about that, myself, but I would still like for you to come."

"I wouldn't miss it," she said walking away from the table. "Now, eat your pancakes before they get cold."

Frank poured syrup over the top of the stack and began to eat.

"They're coming to see you today," said George.

Frank turned and stared at his friend. "What the hell are you talking about?"

"The egg people. You mentioned that nobody has asked to buy your farm. They are coming to see you today."

"How do you know?" asked Frank as he stuck a forkful of food in his mouth.

"I have my sources."

"Sources? What sources could you possibly have?"

"Just never mind. I've got my people who keep me informed."

"Your people? Shit, George. Either tell me, or I'll put a lump on your head."

"Do you know Yancy Tucker's aunt who works over at the feed mill? Well, she said that Bess Roger's sister heard Ben Hicks say that he overheard a conversation between two of them egg people, and that they were coming over to see you."

Frank stared at his friend for a moment and then said, "So, that's your people. Right, George?"

"Well, yeah. Kind of."

"George, if you took all those people you mentioned and put them all together the only thing that would be less than their combined number of teeth would be their combined I.Q."

"Well, that's not all together true. Ben Hicks graduated from high school. At least, that's what he tells everybody."

Frank spent the next few moments eating his breakfast. "Tell me, George. Everyone seems to have turned against me except you. Why is that?"

"I'm a part of the information network. Hell, if I don't stay friends with you, how's anybody going to know what's going on."

"Good point," said Frank. "Well, be sure to pass this tidbit along. I think those egg people are dishonest, and furthermore, I think they were responsible for Merle Hensen's death."

"Good God, Frank. What makes you think that?"

"I was out at Hensen's farm yesterday and saw that wheel that came off Merle's tractor, and I can tell you that Merle wasn't the last one to monkey with that wheel."

"And I suppose you're going to tell me what you found."

"Sure, I'll tell you. At first, it was so obvious that I didn't see it. You know. Can't see the forest for the trees, but suddenly, there it was."

"There what was?"

"The wheel had been wiped clean. Not a trace of grease or dirt. In fact, it looked like a new wheel."

George stared at his friend. "Hell, that's enough evidence for me," he said. "Let's lock 'em up and throw away the key."

"George, when's the last time you ever saw any farmer clean the grease from the wheel of a tractor? You'll never see it. They all believe that it protects it and keeps the dirt away from the hub. Merle was no exception. In the last forty years that he owned that machine, he never once cleaned the wheels. Why, all of a sudden, would they be wiped clean?"

"I don't know. Maybe, Merle was into spring housecleaning?"

"Irma told me that two men in suits from the egg factory arrived just after I left. I don't know how they did it or when, but I know they loosened that wheel after Merle tightened it. They probably left fingerprints and decided to wipe the wheel completely clean."

"If you're so sure of this, why don't you go to the law?"

"I'm afraid they would laugh me out of the place. No, I'm sure that's not enough evidence to even talk to them, but it's enough for me."

George took a long sip from his coffee cup and returned it to the table. "If you're right about all this, you know what that means don't you?"

"It means that I'm in trouble."

"That's exactly right," said George. "You need to be real careful, my friend. Really careful."

Frank picked up his coffee cup and examined the contents. He could see that it was no longer hot, so he set it back down with a disgusted look. "I think you're right, George," he said. "Unfortunately, I think you're right."

Ⅎ Ⅎ Ⅎ

It was late in the morning when Frank stepped out the back door. His truck had less than a thousand miles since its last oil change, but it had been over five months. Frank decided it was time to do the job.

He walked across the backyard and entered the garage. Hanging over the workbench was a small plastic pan used for catching dirty oil as it drained from the engine. He grabbed a wrench hanging next to it and started for the truck.

Frank got down on one knee and slid the pan under the truck. He, then, rolled over onto his back and slid under the vehicle. He noticed traces of oil dripping down the sides of the oil pan and decided that on his next trip to town, he would talk to Sam about replacing the gasket that had gone bad.

He tightened the wrench around the drain plug and gave it a turn. It soon broke free and after several more turns, the plug fell from the hole and landed in the pan below. A strong and steady stream of black liquid emerged from the outlet.

Frank heard vehicles pulling into his driveway. They stopped just behind his truck, their engines still idling. He could hear doors opening and closing as he began to slide from under the truck.

"Mr. Watson?"

Frank got to his feet and wiped his hands with a rag that was stuffed in his back pocket. Three men stood in front of him. Two were wearing dark suits and the third, who was considerably older, was wearing pinstriped pants that belonged to a suit and a dress shirt with no tie. Parked in his driveway was a black Cadillac and a white pickup.

"I'm Frank Watson," he said still wiping his hands.

"My name is Mike Ballinger," he said extending his hand.

Frank paused and then took his hand. "What's on your mind?" he asked.

"Mr. Watson, I couldn't help but notice what a good-looking truck you have here," he said running his hand down one side of the vehicle.

"You drove all the way out here to tell me that?"

"No, sir, I didn't," he said with a grin. "But if I did, it certainly would be worth the trip. Mr. Watson, I can see that you're the kind of man that would prefer that I come straight to the point, so that's just what I'm going to do.

Mr. Watson, I represent a large organization that is interested in buying your farm."

"I'm sure you do, but I'm not interested."

"Mr. Watson, my people are willing to give you top dollar for your land."

"Not interested."

"Now, Frank. May I call you Frank?"

"You can call me Mr. Watson."

The man stared at Frank for a moment, smiled, and kicked at a stone next to his feet. "Mr. Watson, we seemed to have got off to a bad start. I don't think you realize the amount of money we will be bringing to your small town, and from what I've seen, you could use it."

"We've survived this long without you and your money, and I imagine we'll get along without you in the future."

"Mr. Watson, I need to ask you a question. Why are you so dead set against us? We're not monsters. We're just a group of people trying to expand our business."

"You ain't going to like my answer, Mr. Ballinger. If the people of this town don't like my thinking, I'm damn sure positive you ain't going to like it."

"Try me. I'm an open-minded man."

"Well, it's real simple. I think you're screwing around with nature. You're asking for problems by sticking that many chickens in a small area. It just ain't right. No good can come out of it. I know that for certain."

Mr. Ballinger looked over at one of the men who was with him and then back at Frank. "What do you think will happen?"

"I'm not sure. I guess that's part of the reason I'm against it."

"Are you concerned about the excessive manure?"

"That problem did occur to me."

"We sell it to the farmers in the area, and they spread it on their fields. Best fertilizer in the world, and we get rid of a problem."

"What happens when the farmers have enough? Where do you spread your crap then?"

"Mr. Watson, let me assure that we have done our homework. We've been doing this for many years, and we won't create any problems."

"I know you won't create any problems for me because I'm not selling my farm. Now, if you and your two friends will excuse me, I have work to do."

"No problem, Mr. Watson. We'll be leaving, but let me just say that you'll be getting an offer on your farm in the mail in just a few days. I'm sure you'll agree that it's a generous offer, and as a signing bonus, we are prepared to throw in the new pick up that you see here. In fact, we'd like to leave it with you for a few days while you make up your mind. After all, it's already in your name."

"It's what?"

"Technically, it belongs to you, so why not drive it for a while?"

Frank took two steps towards the vehicle and stopped. "No, no," he said waving his hand. "Take it with you. I don't want that thing around here, do you understand?"

"No problem," said Ballinger walking towards the car. The two men in suits climbed into the truck and started the engine. "Keep watching your mail, and we'll be back to see you after you've read our offer. Have a nice day." The two vehicles backed onto the road and drove away.

8 A MEMORIAL DAY PICNIC

The warm winds of spring blew across the rich and fertile farmlands ushering in another season of planting and harvesting. Even though there were weeks before summer officially began, Memorial Day had always represented the beginning of summer to the people of Springfield. They celebrated the day with a parade down Main Street and cookouts in virtually every backyard in town.

Frank uncovered his gas grill and lifted the lid. The grate was covered with the char and ash of last year's barbecues. He picked up a spatula and began to scrape off the residue.

Memorial Day was one of Frank's favorite holidays. It meant the beginning of the warm days of summer, of baseball games and picnics, and more importantly, a reunion of his family. It was a day that Frank greatly anticipated especially since Ida died leaving him alone.

The first of his two children arrived around eleven. As Frank expected, it was Betty, the older of the two. She had always been the punctual one. If she had been less than an hour early, Frank would have been worried.

Frank had always been proud of both his children. He tried never to show that he favored one over the other, but there was no doubt that he had a special place in his heart for his first born.

Betty Watson had always had ambitious goals and aspirations, even as a child. Nobody in town doubted her when she declared that she would be the first woman president. To many, it was just a matter of waiting.

She did become a successful attorney, her career taking her far away from home. She had a busy life and enjoyed her work, but looked forward to the summer holidays back home on the farm.

"Hi, Dad," she said as she fell into his open arms.

"Welcome home, Daughter," he said. "How have you been?"

"Good. Real good. How are you, Dad? You're looking good."

"Never felt better. In fact, this is the best I've felt in years."

"Could it have anything to do with the company you keep now? By the way, is she here yet?" she asked peering into the windows of the house. "Am I going to meet this woman who is probably younger than me."

"Yes, you'll meet her, and she's three years older than you."

"Oh, my God! Three whole years! She's practically in Depends!"

"Be nice."

"Hey, Dad, do you love her?"

"Well, we have a relationship that..."

"Do you love her, Dad?"

"Well, yes. I suppose I do."

"Then, that's all that matters. Life's too short to worry about the details."

"Where's that fellow you've been seeing? You know…the one with his own jet."

Betty shook her head. "I knew he was too good to be true. The reason he had a jet was to get him back home to his wife and kids."

"Oh, no."

"That's all right, Dad. I have a real problem with a guy who wears women's underwear. So, what can I do, Pop? I've been looking forward to this day for a long time."

"Women's underwear?"

"Says he's allergic to cotton. Is that possible? Hey, that's enough about him."

"Did he wear a bra, too?"

"Dad!"

"There's a pan of chicken inside. Go get it." Betty started for the door. "And if he did, what size cup did he wear?" She gave her father a quick look and disappeared into the house.

Frank leaned over and turned a knob on the tank of gas. He, then, pushed a button on the front of the grill, and fire roared to life inside. Betty returned carrying a pan of food.

"You love to cook outside, don't you Dad?"

"Amazing, isn't it? Must be a sign of the times. Everything is backwards these days."

"What do you mean, Dad?"

"Used to be a time when we ate indoors and shit outside."

Betty glanced down at the grill and back at her father. "You're a crazy man. You know that, don't you?"

"I've been told that by smarter people than you."

Just then, an older model station wagon stopped just behind Betty's Grand Cherokee. Both back doors opened even before the car was completely stopped, and two young boys got out. Without closing the doors behind them, they ran wildly across the backyard towards the barn.

"Batten down the hatches," said Frank.

A tall, slim-figured woman got out of the passenger side, talking incessantly. She was still leaning over barking orders to the driver who was still behind the wheel.

"I don't know what he did wrong in life, but he's sure paying for it now," said Frank.

"I wonder why he doesn't just leave her," said Betty. Divorce can't be any worse than living with her."

"I don't think she would allow it," said Frank. "Don't forget. Lloyd lost his testicles a long time ago, and unfortunately, Helen found them."

"Hello, there!" shouted the woman beside the car. She leaned over and put her head inside the door. "Are you going to get out of the car, Lloyd?"

The door opened, and a frail man wearing matching shorts and shirt slowly got out of the car. "Do you want me to check on the boys, Helen?"

"They'll be fine," she said. "Besides, it's just a barn. What can they destroy in a barn?"

Summer Harvest

Lloyd paused and stared at the building. "It really worries me when they're quiet, Helen."

"Dad, how are you?" asked Helen as she kissed him on the cheek. Before he could reply, she turned to the woman standing next to him. "Betty, you're looking beautiful. Did you ever find Mister Right? Lloyd, go check on the boys. They're much too quiet. There might be some livestock in that barn, and God knows what those two might do."

"Be right back, Pop," said Lloyd with a slight wave of his hand and started for the barn.

"Did you ever think about medication for those two?" asked Frank.

"What are you talking about? They are on medication. The doctor wasn't going to do it until he had two nurses and a receptionist quit because of them. He couldn't write a prescription fast enough. So, tell me, Dad. Is she here? I can't wait to meet the little woman who caught your eye. Have you seen her yet, Betty?"

"I don't think..."

"Well, what have those two been into?" shouted Helen at Lloyd who was walking slowly towards the group of people.

"Hi, Pop," he said shaking his father's hand. "Hi, Sis."

"Hi, Lloyd," she said kissing him on the cheek.

"Well, what have they been doing?"

Lloyd turned to his wife. "Your sons have already killed a rat."

"In that short of time? That's not possible."

"They not only killed it, but have it half dissected already."

"Oh, good grief," said Helen. "What are they planning to do with it?"

"I don't know. I told them that we were having chicken up here at the house."

"Oh, Lloyd, they wouldn't eat the thing," she said. She turned to Frank and then back to her husband. "They wouldn't, would they?"

"We never did find out what happened to Smokey, the cat."

"You two aren't planning on having any more kids, are you?" asked Frank.

"Helen had her tubes tied after Kevin was born," said Lloyd. "I went in for a vasectomy as well. Wasn't taking any chances."

"Not that either operation was necessary," said Helen with a sneer.

"All right, said Frank. "I'll get started on the chicken while you two bring the potato salad and beans outside."

"What can I do, Pop?" asked Lloyd.

"You can stand right there and tell me how you've been," said Frank carefully placing the pieces of chicken on the hot grill. "What's been going on in your life. Are you still working at that cardboard factory?"

"Still there," said Lloyd. "Got a promotion last month."

"Oh, ya. What are you doing now?"

"I get to operate one of the machines instead of carrying baling wire all over the place. Hell, I get fifty cents more an hour and get to sit down as well. Just getting to sit down was raise enough, but I ain't telling them that."

"Did you ever finish building that airplane you had started? My God, you had that thing over half done the last time I saw it. I've been waiting for a call from you to take me up in the thing."

"No, I had to scrap it and the idea."

"Why, son? What happened?"

"Just too many things going on. That's all."

"Helen made you get rid of it, didn't she?"

"Well, it was taking up the whole backyard, and it was costing me a lot of money."

Frank lifted the top on the grill and began turning the pieces of meat. "Jesus, son. I can't believe you."

"You can't believe what?"

Frank dropped the fork that was in his hand and closed the lid to the grill. "You can't let her do that to you, son. It's just not right."

"What's not right?"

"You can't let her take your dreams away from you, son. Every man needs a dream, and she's making damn sure you don't have one. You can't let her do it, Lloyd."

The back door opened and Helen stepped outside carrying a bowl of potato salad. "What are you two talking about? You look way too serious."

The two men exchanged glances. Lloyd turned to his wife and said, "We were just talking about..."

"When's your little friend coming, Dad?" she asked setting the bowl on the table. "I can't wait to meet her."

"I told her to be here around noon."

"How convenient," she said. "She'll get here just in time to sit down to eat. Lloyd, you come with me and help bring out the rest of the stuff." Lloyd stared at his father for a moment, turned, and followed his wife into the house.

It was just before noon when an older model Escort pulled into the driveway and parked behind the row of cars. A young woman emerged from the vehicle and walked over to the group already sitting around the picnic table.

"There she is," muttered Frank and got to his feet. He gave her a kiss on the cheek and led her to the table of people.

"Pepper, I'd like you to meet my family," Frank announced. "This is my daughter, Betty, and this is my son, Lloyd and his wife, Helen." Frank led her to the other side of the table. "These are my two grandsons. Don't get too close because if they should happen to bite you, there's all those shots to go through."

Pepper leaned over to the two young boys. "Hi, my name is Pepper. What's your names?"

"Are you a thief?" asked one of the boys.

"A thief? Why would you ask me something like that?"

"My mother said you're stealing the inheritance away from us. Why else would anyone date an old geezer like Grandpa?"

Pepper straightened back up. She turned to Frank with a blank stare.

"Precious, aren't they?" asked Frank. All eyes turned to Helen.

"Kids say the darndest things," she said. "I don't know where he gets half the stuff that he says."

"But Mom!" shouted one of the boys. "You said..."

"Okay, Pepper, why don't you come over here and sit down. We can clear a spot for you. You two little nitwits move over and let the lady sit down."

Bowls of food were passed around the table as everyone helped themselves. Silence fell on the small gathering of people as they hungrily devoured the food on the table.

Helen was the first to finish her piece of chicken. She wiped her hands on a napkin as she leaned back on the bench. It was obvious to everyone that a large piece of chicken was stuck between two of her teeth, and she began to make sucking noises as she tried to unsuccessfully dislodge it. She increased the intensity and frequency of the effort until everyone else had stopped eating and had turned their attention to her.

She was becoming increasingly frustrated with the stubborn piece of food but didn't seem the least bit embarrassed with the attention she was receiving. She thrust her index finger in her mouth and doggedly picked at the chunk of food. "Damn you. Come loose," she mumbled around the finger that was now buried in her mouth.

"Got 'cha, you little shit!" she said and withdrew her finger. She inhaled a large volume of air and with extreme force, she expelled the unwanted piece of food from her mouth. It sailed across the table and stuck on Frank's knit polo shirt.

Frank glanced down to the front of his shirt and then at Helen. "Nice shot, Helen," he said. "Does this mean that you want me to put it back on the grill or did you just want to share your food with me?"

"Sorry, Frank," she said as she ran her tongue over her teeth in search of any more foreign objects.

"Not a problem," he said as he brushed the substance from his shirt.

"So, tell me, Frank, how long have you and What's-Her-Name been seeing each other?" asked Helen.

"Pepper!" shouted Lloyd.

"What?"

"Pepper! The woman's name is Pepper!"

"How long have you and Pepper been seeing each other?"

"You're in luck, Helen," said Frank. "We just started seeing each other, so if you don't approve, we can end this thing right here and now, and nobody gets hurt."

"Oh, don't get me wrong," she said. "I think it's great when a man your age thinks he still has what it takes."

The smile on Frank's face disappeared. He started to say something and then leaned over his plate to finish eating his meal.

"Helen, just change the subject," whispered Lloyd.

Silence fell on the table of people. Helen began to eat the food remaining on her plate stuffing large forkfuls of food into her mouth.

"So, Frank, does this mean you're finally over Ida?"

"Helen!" shouted Lloyd. "That's going too far!"

Frank dropped his fork onto his plate. He got to his feet and threw his napkin on the table. "Helen, all the years I've known you, we've never seen eye-to-eye on anything. I've endured your insults and rude behavior because you're my son's wife, but you crossed the line today.

I would have thought that even someone as irritating and nasty as you wouldn't have even considered mentioning Ida like that." Frank began to walk away, stopped, and turned around. "I swear to God, Helen," he said pointing a finger at her. "If you were to look in the dictionary under the word, Bitch, your picture would be there!" He turned and stormed away. Pepper got up from her seat and followed him.

"Jeez!" said Helen. "Aren't we being a little sensitive?"

Frank walked around to the front of the house and sat down on the porch swing. He eased it into motion as he stared across the cornfield. Pepper fell into the rhythm of the swing and sat down beside him. Neither spoke as they nudged the swing into a gentle back-and-forth motion.

"I'm sorry about that back there," said Frank. "I shouldn't let her get to me."

"I'm surprised that no one has hit her yet!"

"She's always been a nasty person. You'd think I would be used to her by now. She's always made offensive remarks about everything and everybody, but when it comes to Ida, I have to draw the line.

Ida never said anything bad about Helen. Even when Helen would attack Ida, she would still say nothing. Even after a whole day of Helen, I would ask Ida why she never said anything to her, and she would reply that it was not the kind of thing that Jesus would want her to do."

"Ida must have been a saint," said Pepper.

"I told her that Jesus, himself, wouldn't put up with Helen, and do you know what she said to that? She told me that Jesus forgives Helen and I should, too. Can you believe that?"

"Ida sounds too good to be true. Was she always like that?"

"Did you ever know anyone to run over a squirrel and then take it to the vet? That was Ida."

"So, Frank, where do we go from here? You've got a small group of people behind your house that should be done eating about now. I'm sure they're wondering whether to go home, go for seconds, or wind their watches."

Frank turned to her with a slight grin. "My God, I feel like an idiot. Why do I let her get to me like that?"

"Well, Frank, I've known her for less than an hour, and I'm already wondering how much hit men are these days."

"This is stupid," said Frank getting to his feet. "I can't leave those people back there like that. Let's go back and join the party."

The two people walked around to the back of the house. As they approached the group, it was obvious that a heated debate was in progress. Lloyd and Betty were pointing at each other and speaking in raised voices. Silence returned as Frank and Pepper stopped at the end of the table.

"I want to apologize to all of you for my outburst and loss of temper," he said. He, then, turned to Helen. "I'm sorry, Helen. What I said was wrong and should never been said."

Helen said nothing. She stared blankly straight ahead, occasionally glancing at the man standing in front of her. Lloyd gently nudged her with his elbow and whispered something in her ear. She began to speak and then fell silent. She glanced at her husband and then back at Frank.

"I'm sorry, too," she blurted and looked away.

"Dad, we were just discussing the fact that you have this golden opportunity to sell the farm," said Lloyd. "I know it's none of our business, but is it true that you refuse to sell?"

"That pretty much sums it up," said Frank. "Why do you ask?"

"Pop, do you realize what a great opportunity this is? Farmland is not exactly a great commodity right now. Prices are dropping every day. If you have an offer, now is the time to sell."

Frank took a seat at the table. "Lloyd, pardon my asking, but why the sudden concern for my financial well-being?"

"Lloyd wants to be sure that you leave the biggest chunk of inheritance possible," said Betty.

"That's not fair, Betty, and you know it," said Lloyd angrily.

"Not fair? You just said that if he didn't sell it now, it probably wouldn't be worth half as much by the time we got it."

"I think we all know that neither one of us has any intention of keeping the farm. We don't know anything about farming and could care less. Why not sell it now and get top dollar? It just makes sense."

"What you do with this farm after I'm gone is your business," said Frank looking at both of his children. "God knows there's nothing I can do about it after I'm gone, but until that time, there's no way that I would ever consider selling it."

"It's just a piece of land, Dad," said Lloyd. "That's all it is. If you're too old to work the land and we have no interest, sell it and turn it into cash."

"You know, I always dreamed that one of you two would take an interest in the farm and that it would pass on to the next generation. This farm has been in the family for over a hundred and fifty years. There have been many Watson's doing many things to hang onto this farm. It has survived flood, fire, bad weather, and bank closures and is still owned by a Watson. Generations of Watson's have worked the land and managed to rear a family. Their blood, their sweat, and ultimately their bodies are buried in that soil nurturing it so that future generations can enjoy the same kind of life that it has always offered. All the generations that have come before have never considered it an inheritance. It has always been more than just a piece of property. It has been a legacy passed from one generation to another. I consider it more than just a legacy. I think of it as a gift of love. It was a gift when my father gave it to me and a gift when his father passed it on to him. It is now approaching the end of the second century of being in the family and will soon be entrusted to you two. The fate of the farm will rest on your shoulders. All I ask is that you do what you think is right. That's all. Whatever is the right thing to do should be your only concern."

There was a solemn silence as the group of people respectfully listened to Frank. "Did you ever consider selling the farm, Dad?" asked Betty.

"Many times," he responded. "There were times I didn't think I was going to make it. Bad weather can kill an entire year's crop, you know. But the legacy had been passed onto me. It was my responsibility, and I was not going to disappoint the voices from the past."

"Voices? You heard voices?" asked Pepper.

"Indeed, I did, as did all those who came before me. It maybe the rustling leaves as a gentle wind blows through a field of corn or the lonely whippoorwill on a summer night. I can hear the echoes from the past when the midnight train rumbles over the Boggs Creek trestle, or the noises that this old house makes on a quiet night that sound like voices from the many graves of our ancestors of long ago.

Yes, the voices are there, if you know where to listen. They haunted me, yet guided me to do the right thing. It will soon be your turn to do the right thing. If selling the farm should happen to be the right thing, then it will be your job to do just that. But don't ask me to do it for you. This land means more to me than any amount of money. You'll have to decide for yourselves when the time comes."

Frank fell silent as he stared across a field of wheat. The others took quick, furtive glances at each other not really knowing what to say.

"All this talk is beginning to depress me," said Betty breaking the silence. "Chances are, you're going to outlive us all anyway, so all we're doing here today is ruining a perfectly good Memorial Day."

"Spoken with the diplomacy of a truly good lawyer," said Frank. "How 'bout we clean up this mess and make some homemade ice cream? After all, what would Memorial Day be without it?"

"Sounds great to me," said Pepper.

"Me, too," said Betty.

"Let's go," said Lloyd, and they all grabbed something on the table and got to their feet.

"I'm allergic to homemade ice cream," said Helen. "Do you happen to have anything else?"

All eyes fell on Helen and then turned to Frank. He smiled and slowly shook his head. "Ya, Helen," he said. "I think I have something in the freezer for you. After all, I knew you were coming."

9 DAD REMEMBERS

There were dark, angry clouds the next morning as Frank drove into town. It was just beginning to rain when Frank parked his truck in front of the restaurant. He climbed out of the vehicle and walked into the building. Silence fell on the long table of men as he walked slowly towards the rear of the place.

"Good morning, gentlemen," he said cautiously.

"Morning, Frank," came one timid voice.

Frank poured himself a cup of coffee and sat down in his normal spot. "Good morning, George," he said.

"Morning, Frank. Ain't you the popular one? You still got it, Frank. You still got that old charisma. You can still make a room full of people turn mute."

"And these are my friends," said Frank. "Hard to believe, isn't it?"

"Hell, I think they even have something against me just because I still talk to you."

"What were they saying before I came in?"

"I couldn't hear much," said George. "They were keeping it kind of quiet. Guess they figured I'd tell you what they were saying."

"Isn't America wonderful?"

"Where the buffalo roam."

"Good morning, Frank," said Pepper setting a plate of food in front of George. "The usual?"

"Yes, please."

"I did manage to pick up one thing though," said George. "Do you remember Howard Bower, the guy who went to our school for a couple years?"

"Yeah, I remember him. He had the face that looked like a rodent. We kept bringing cheese to school for him."

"That's the guy," said George. "We even put a mouse trap in his locker. Well, anyway, this guy owns a farm in Jefferson County, not too far from the egg factory. One of the guys ran into him the other day, and I guess he's not too happy with those people."

"Did you hear any details?"

"No, but I have a feeling that there is more to that egg business than we've been told."

"I'm convinced that there's something sinister about these people, and I'm even more convinced that you're going to have problems when you stick millions of chickens in a small piece of land."

"Here you go, Honey," said Pepper sliding a plate of food in front of Frank.

"Thank you, darlin'," said Frank staring at the plate. "I can't decide which is prettier; a plate of bacon and eggs or the waitress who brought it."

"Thank God, I didn't throw on that extra strip of bacon, or there would probably been no contest."

"You know there is something you can do to give yourself an edge," said Frank.

"And what might that be?" she asked as she filled his coffee cup.

"Change your perfume to eau du bacon, and I'll follow you anywhere."

"You're right, Frank," said Pepper. "That's every girls' dream to smell like a pig." She turned a glanced at the table of men and then back at Frank. "You be careful, Frank. I manage to hear things being said, and you're not too popular right now."

"That goes for you, too," said Frank. "Don't forget you're the wanton hussy who is seeing the evil Frank Watson."

"Sorry, but these country hicks don't scare me," she said with a smile. "I grew up in a neighborhood where the weak were literally eaten. By the way, have you learned anything more about this egg business?"

"No, but I think I'm going to pay a visit to an old friend in Jefferson County right after I see Dad this afternoon. I think it's about time I got to the bottom of this matter," he said, as he thrust another forkful of food into his mouth.

"Frank, my friend," came a voice from the other end of the table. "How are you. We don't see much of you anymore."

Scott Fields

"Willard? Is that you?" asked Frank. "Excuse my confusion, but I really didn't know you cared."

"Frank, you hurt my feelings. How many years have we known each other?"

"Get to the point, Willard," said Frank. "Your attempt at being nice is really unbecoming. I prefer you in your natural state of being a snot."

"Are you going to sell your farm, or not?"

"I have no intentions of selling, and you people are crazy for being sucked in by these people."

"Frank, be reasonable. These people have a lot of money and want to share some of it with us."

"Willard, do you have any idea what it's like to have millions of chickens confined to a small chunk of land?"

"No, I don't, Frank. Do you?"

"No, but I plan to find out. I'm going over to Jefferson County this afternoon and talk to some people who have had an egg farm already. I'm anxious to see if they're as enthusiastic about it now as they were before they came to the area."

"You do that, Frank, and maybe you'll soon see what a great opportunity this is. This is the chance of a lifetime, Frank, and if we don't act right now, these good people are going to move on to some other town."

"These good people. Jesus, Willard, I can't believe their money has blinded you that much. These good people, as you call them, are as shady as can be."

"And I suppose you have some proof of this, or is this just some feeling you have?"

"Didn't you ever wonder about Merle Hensen's death? Didn't it seem a little odd to you?"

"Oh, for Christ's sakes, Frank," said Willard. "You think that these people killed Merle Hensen? What do you think happened? Do you think they rolled his tractor over on top of him? Come on, Frank. Do you have any idea how this sounds to the rest of us?"

"I'm telling you, Willard, those people had something to do with Merle's death. Hell, even the Sheriff is still investigating his death."

"Christ, Frank. Sheriff Boggs is running for re-election this fall. He's got to look like he knows what he's doing. If it wasn't for getting elected, he would have closed this case a long time ago and would be over at Bernice Thompson's house laying the pipe to her."

"I didn't know that Boggs was having an affair with Bernice," said one of the men.

"Tell me, Frank," said Willard. "Do you have any proof that they killed Merle? Some kind of eye witness or evidence that you're holding back?"

Frank said nothing. He stared intently at the man speaking to him.

"Well, Frank, I'm waiting."

"No, Willard, I don't have any proof."

"Well, that's just great, Frank. You want us to give up on some serious money coming into this town because you have a hunch about these people?"

"You know, Willard, the town is doing just fine without these people and their money," said Frank. "In fact, ever since you lost your bid for re-election as mayor, things couldn't be better."

"Come on, Frank. You don't have to get personal."

"Yes, I do, Willard!" shouted Frank getting to his feet. He pulled a five-dollar bill from his pocket and threw it on the table. "You got personal when this conversation began, and I've had enough of it!" He stormed across the room and grabbed the handle to the front door. He turned and looked at Willard. "By the way, Willard. I understand that Sheriff Bogg's cruiser has been seen in front of your house when you're out of town. Have a nice day," he said and walked out the door.

৪ ৪ ৪

It was just after nine o'clock when Frank's back door opened and closed.

"Jesus, Frank, you've done it now!" exclaimed Toad as she walked into the kitchen.

"My God, you're an hour early. The grapevine must be on fire."

"Did you really tell Willard Miller to kiss your butt?"

"Aren't you going to make coffee?"

"I can only stay for a minute. Well, did you?"

"Did I what?"

"Did you tell Willard to kiss your ass?"

"No, not really," he said. "At least, not in so many words. The thought was there, though, and I'm real sure that Willard got the message."

"Well, I'll tell you one thing, Mr. Watson," said Toad. "You don't dig your heels in very often, but when you do, you sure know how to pick your fights. Not many people take on the whole town."

"I seemed to have stirred up a hornets' nest. That's for sure."

"Well, I have to be going," she said opening the door. "Are you going to see your father today?"

"Yes, I am. In fact, I'll be leaving in a few minutes because when I'm done there, I'm going to run over to Jefferson County. I need to talk to some people over there about their egg factory. Kind of curious about what they think of it."

"You be careful!" she said sternly. "There's a lot of people who have scratched your name from their Christmas card list. By the way, if your father is in his right mind give him my regards."

"I'll do that."

"See ya," she said and closed the door behind her.

ಐ ಐ ಐ

Frank pulled into the nursing home parking lot as he had done many times before. The rain had all but stopped leaving behind a cold and dark sky. Frank entered the building and made his way down the hall. There was the usual screaming and crying as he walked by the open doors. The air seemed to be permanently stained with the offensive smells that emanated from the rooms.

Frank turned into his father's room and stood in the open doorway. His roommate was lying half out of bed with his head nearly touching the floor. With his eyes closed and his mouth gaping open, he had a look of death upon him.

Frank turned and walked over to his father's bed. He was lying on his back in the middle of his bed; his eyes open staring at the ceiling.

"Hi, Pop," greeted Frank with a bounce in his voice. "How are you today?"

The old man didn't move his eyes unflinching. Frank could feel his pulse quicken as he moved closer and took his father's hand. He was relieved with the touch of warmth coming from his body. He leaned over and stared at the old man's eyes that seemed not to blink.

"Dad," he said with a louder voice. "It's your son, Frank. Can you hear me?"

Still nothing. Frank moved even closer. "Dad, are you all right?" He smothered the old man's limp and flaccid hand between both of his and gently kissed him on the cheek.

He slowly pulled back and stared into his father's eyes. A lone tear streaked down the old man's face and disappeared into his snow-white hair.

"Dad, talk to me," he said gripping his hand tighter. "What's the matter? Don't you feel well? Whatever it is, Dad, I can fix it. I promise."

The old man slowly turned his head until he was facing his son. His face was sad, the kind of sadness that comes when the spirit of life leaves the body. "This time it can't be fixed, son," he said with a blank stare. "It's too late."

"What do you mean by that, Dad? What's too late? What can't be fixed?"

The old man turned his head towards the ceiling again. "I wasted so much of my life. So many days wasted. Dear God, if I could do it all again."

"Do what again? Dad, talk to me."

"When you come down to the end, you know. When the day slips into night, you know, too. Days seem to rush by like a stranger brushing by you in a crowd," he said and turned to face Frank once again. His face looked relaxed now. He grinned slightly as he stared into his son's eyes. "I'm standing on the edge of the abyss, son. I was scared, but no more. There's so many things I wish I could undo, and so many things that need to be said, but there's no time."

"What are you talking about, Dad. You'll be fine. You'll see. I always said that you will outlive us all."

"You know, son, when you're young, each day is like a blade of grass. You pluck one, and it's never missed. There are countless others to take its place. Then, in the twilight of your years, each day is precious, to be revered and regarded as a gift from God." The old man turned slightly in his bed for comfort. The grin vanished from his face. "The years that pass steal precious youth leaving you crippled and soured with regrets of things undone and others done without thought. We are the victims of our own decisions, the product of our own destiny. We toil hard all our lives, and our reward is a body that withers and dies.

Well, I fooled 'em son. I fooled 'em good. My reward is yet to come. My reward is in the hereafter when I'm reunited with your mother. There's nothing left for me here on earth, son. I love you very much, Frank, but I miss your mother. I've missed her every day for a lot of years. So, please forgive me when I tell you that I welcome death with open arms. I truly believe that I was put on this earth to care and look out for your mother, and I can't be happy wondering if she's all right. I need to go to her, son. I know in my heart that she needs me."

Frank removed the handkerchief from his back pocket and wiped away the tears that were flowing down his face. "Dad, please don't do this to me. You've always been the rock in my life. It's hard for me to see you like this. To see you lying in bed day after day, your body wasting away was hard enough, but to see you lose hope and the spirit to live is too much for me."

"Lose hope? No, son. Don't cry for me. It's only my body that is about to die. My spirit will go on. Be happy for me, for soon I will be free of this wretched, worn out body, and will soon make that fateful step, the step that all humans rue but inevitably must make."

Frank stepped back and wiped his eyes once again as he stared at his father lying in bed. The old man turned his head once again and stared at the ceiling. Frank took several deep breaths and once more grabbed his father's hand.

"You're not thinking right, Pop," he said. "Your head is all messed up. In fact, I've never seen you quite this bad." He squeezed his hand tightly with one hand and held him by the shoulder with the other. "You'll feel better tomorrow. I promise.

Tomorrow, you'll think differently. You'll be your old self again, calling me names and wanting to get out of here. You'll see."

The old man's eyes seemed hollow and lifeless as he stared at the ceiling without blinking.

Frank's body suddenly shuddered, as a chill seemed to penetrate his very soul. He glanced around the room as if someone had entered. There was no one there. Even his father's roommate had grown silent. There was a stillness that Frank had never known. Death was settling on the room like a shroud over a lifeless body. Frank gazed at this once strong and virile man who was at the end of his life and felt both sorrow and contentment. He felt sorrow for himself and for the passing of an era, and contentment for his father and his ultimate fulfillment of his destiny.

"Hey, Pop. Do you remember when I was only ten years old and my dog, Bullet got killed. I was devastated. I had never experienced death, and my first time had to be my favorite dog. You were there for me, Dad. As always, you made things right. I never could be the rock of a man that you were. I always wanted my kids to idolize me like I did you, but it was never quite the same." Frank ran his hand through his hair and shook his head as if freeing himself of something. "God, how I looked up to you."

The old man remained unchanged; his eyes fixed on an undefined spot.

"I know you can hear me, Pop. I just wish you would come back to me."

Still nothing.

"When Ida died, I didn't think I could go on, but you were there, Pop. You were there. I don't know what I would have done without you."

The old man did not move.

"I have to go, Pop. I have something to do, but I'll be back again tomorrow. Okay, Pop? You'll feel better tomorrow, and we'll talk. Okay, Pop?" Frank leaned over and kissed his father on the cheek. "I love you, Dad," he said and turned to walk away.

He was nearly to the door when he heard his father say, "Son, come back here." He turned and walked back to his father's bed. Frank felt relief and a feeling of restored hope as he looked at his father's broad smile and eyes that seemed to be laughing.

"What is it, Pop?"

"That sixteenth birthday present, the one that you can't seem to remember?"

"Yes."

"It was a 1949 Ford pick-up truck."

"You remembered! I can't believe it! You're going to be all right, Dad. I just know it. I always said that when the day came you remembered that, your memory was restored and you were on the road to recovery."

"Whatever happened to that truck?"

"I still have it. Everyone thinks I'm crazy, but I still drive it after all these years."

"That's good, Son," he said patting Frank on the back of the hand. "That's real good."

"Greatest day of my life, the day you brought that truck home. I'll never forget it. I was so happy. I swore that day that I would keep it forever, and, so far, I've kept that promise."

The two men grew silent as they stared at one another. Frank was puzzled. He saw in his father's face a look of serenity and peace. It was an expression that he had never seen before. Suddenly, it hit him. He, finally, understood. "Oh, my God," he muttered. The old man grabbed Frank's hands and held them tightly with his. It was a moment in time that would haunt Frank for the rest of his life. The truth was there in his eyes. The truth was in his smile.

"You're not going to get any better, are you, Dad?"

The old man gazed into his son's eyes, his smile widened. "This is what I want," he said. "This is what I have to do."

Frank eased back slightly still holding onto his father's hands. He said nothing as years of memories suddenly flooded his mind. He smelled the pine as he watched his father place the star atop the Christmas tree. He felt the gentle push as his father launched him on his first solo bicycle ride. He could smell the hot dog that his father handed him at the ballpark as he watched his first major league baseball game. He could feel the coolness of a riverbank as he sat quietly with his father staring excitedly at a red and white bobber floating lazily in the water.

Frank pulled back releasing his hold on his father's hands. For a few more moments, he gazed into the old man's eyes. "I have to go, Pop," he said slowly stepping backwards. "I really must go."

"Good bye, Son," said the old man with a slight wave of his hand.

"Good bye, Dad," he said and turned and walked away.

ಎ ಎ ಎ

The old truck groaned as it turned onto the highway that led out of town. The egg factory was nearly a hundred miles away, and it was already early afternoon. Frank considered turning around and making the trip another day, but he was much too anxious to talk with some of the people who lived near the place.

He was just five miles out of town, when his truck began to labor as it started the long climb up Gamble Hill. It was the only hill for miles around and was noted for its long and gentle approach on one side and the sharp descent on the other. It had always been a particularly dangerous stretch of road. Winter storms of any proportion would most certainly close this part of the highway until salt trucks could improve conditions.

Frank came to the crest of the hill and started his descent. His truck quickly gathered speed. It was a straight road that led down the hill until it reached the base where it took a slight curve to the left.

Frank was halfway down the hill, and his speed was over sixty miles per hour. He tapped his foot on the brake pedal. Nothing. He jammed his foot on the pedal. It was limp; offering no resistance as it depressed all the way to the floor. He pumped it again. Still, nothing.

Frank quickly studied the road ahead. He was going much too fast to make the bend in the road. Lying straight ahead was a ditch on the shoulder of the road, a wire fence, and an open field of wheat. If his truck could survive the sudden jolt from crossing the ditch, he knew that he would eventually come to a stop by coasting through the field just beyond.

His truck hit the bottom of the hill, going over seventy miles per hour. Instead of following the curve in the road, he held on tightly to the steering wheel. The truck left the road. Frank braced himself for it to drop down into the ditch, but it was not to be. He was airborne! For a few brief moments, the old Ford had freed itself of earthly bonds and was aloft without disgrace, carrying its passenger safely over the ditch.

The venerable, old truck came back to earth, thankfully, landing on all four tires at the same time. It rolled uncontrollably in a straight line leaving a path of destruction in its wake. The tender wheat stalks whipped violently at the intruder in a futile effort to slow its journey.

It was about a half-mile into the field of grain before the vehicle finally came to rest. The land was flat, and there was no danger of the truck rolling again.

Frank released his grip from the steering wheel and slowly dropped his hands into his lap. He moved his head and shoulders gently to check for any injury. He felt no pain. He moved his legs. They responded with no obvious problems.

Frank turned the handle on the door of the truck. Nothing. He turned it again and leaned on the door. Still, nothing. He slid across the seat and turned the handle on the passenger's side, and the door sprung open. "That figures," he muttered as he slid out of the truck.

For a moment, he studied the truck looking for any obvious damage. To his surprise, the vehicle appeared to be in good working order despite its brief departure from earth and violent return.

He began to walk back to the road following the path created by the runaway vehicle. The ground was soft from the recent rain, and near the road, Frank found deep trenches formed by the tires as they slammed into the earth.

Within minutes, Frank saw a truck coming his way. It was moving slowly and was obviously heading towards town. He hailed the truck to stop and walked over to the driver's side. There was a man and a woman in the cab with a child between them. He could see that he wouldn't get a ride into town with these people, so he asked them to stop by Wilton's Garage, and instruct Sam to bring his tow truck.

Nearly an hour passed before the old and battered tow truck came to a stop at the side of the road. The door opened, and Samuel climbed out.

"Where in the hell have you been?" asked Frank.

"You know, Frank," said Samuel coming around to the other side of the truck. "As hard as it is for you to believe, I don't just sit around waiting for you to have a problem with your antique truck. I do have other customers."

"Is that any reason to leave me stranded out here?" asked Frank.

"Works for me," he said looking across the field of wheat. "What the hell are you doing way out there. Were you taking a shortcut or something?"

"My brakes went out, you dumb ass, and that's where I ended up," said Frank pointing at the vehicle in the middle of the field.

"Who are you calling a dumb ass, Frank? I'm not the one stranded in the middle of a field of wheat," Samuel said as he stared at the ground near Frank. He looked at the road and then at the broken wire fence. "You went airborne with this old crate, didn't you?"

"You really aren't just another pretty face, are you?" asked Frank with a sneer.

"God, I wish I could have been here to see that," said Sam as he studied the path of the truck.

"Sam, when do you think you can check her for damage?"

"We'll get her back to town, and I'll take a look at her in the morning."

"What about the brakes?"

"I'll check them tomorrow morning."

"Sam, I need to know about those brakes right now."

"Jesus, Frank," he said as he started for the truck. "Could you have picked a worse time? I must have a dozen vehicles that I'm working on right now."

"They'll wait," said Frank. "Just take a quick look for me. That's all. Nothing fancy."

Samuel grumbled as the two men walked across the field. The mechanic circled the truck searching for obvious damage. "She looks pretty good," he said as he raised the hood.

Moments later, he exclaimed, "I found your problem!"

"What is it, Sam?"

"One of your brake lines is loose. In fact, it's barely connected."

"So, what does that mean?"

"It means all of your brake fluid leaked out. That's why you had no brakes."

"Tell me something, Sam. How could that happen? What could possibly go wrong to make a brake line come loose?"

"Frank, that brake line is less than a year old. I know because I'm the one who did your brakes. The only way that line could possibly come loose is if someone deliberately loosened it with a wrench. There's no other way."

"Are you sure?"

"I'm positive," he said. Somebody has been screwing around with your truck, Frank. It looks real clear to me that someone wanted you to have an accident."

"Come on, Sam," said Frank. "Let's get this truck back to your shop. After that, I need you to drop me off at my house. I have some phone calls to make."

It was over an hour later when Sam's tow truck pulled into Frank's driveway. Frank got out of the truck, said a few things to his friend, and entered the back door.

Just as he sat down to pick up the telephone, the back door opened, and in stepped Toad. She was nearly out of breath as if she had run all the way to his house. "Where have you been?" she asked as she gasped for air.

"I had a problem with my truck," he said. "Why do you ask?"

Toad dragged a chair across the floor and positioned it next to her friend. "Frank, the nursing home has been trying to get in touch with you, so they called me instead. I guess I'm in their records as the one to call in an emergency."

Frank slid the phone away from him and dropped his hands into his lap. "What happened?" he asked in a whisper.

"Frank," she said taking one of his hands. "It's your father. He passed away about an hour ago."

Frank dropped his head and leaned back in his chair.

"I'm so sorry, Frank," she said and began to cry.

10 HOWARD OF JEFFERSON COUNTY

Frank felt a sense of relief when the engine of his truck started with just one turn of the key. It had been two weeks since the funeral, and he had not left the house in all that time.

He pulled out of his drive and turned in the direction of the Hainey farm.

It was late in the afternoon on a Saturday, and Frank was on his way to see Pepper. In the last two weeks, he had talked with her on the phone but had asked her to leave him alone in his time of mourning. She didn't quite understand but honored his request.

He parked in the Hainey driveway and got out of his truck. He wasn't halfway to the back steps when the door burst open and Pepper fell into his arms.

"I'm so glad to see you," she said as she kissed him repeatedly.

"My, what a reception," said Frank. "I should stay away from you more often."

"Don't you dare," she said. "Two weeks was enough. You made me a crazy woman."

"Well, hey there young lady," said Frank. "It's a Saturday night. How 'bout you and me taking a ride over to Marion and get something to eat?"

"I'd love to," she said. "Come on in while I get my purse."

Frank stepped into the kitchen while Pepper disappeared into another room. The air was heavy with the smells of dinner on the stove. Irma was standing in front of the stove with a spatula in her hand, and Warren was sitting at the table.

"Well, hello there, Frank," greeted Irma. "How are you doing?"

"Fine, Irma. Just fine."

Frank turned to Warren who was fumbling with a pipe. He had a can of Prince Albert and a pile of kitchen matches next to him and was desperately trying to load the tobacco into the pipe.

"Frank, you came over here awhile back for dinner," said Warren without looking up. "Do you remember that?"

"Yes, Warren. I sure do."

"I couldn't help but notice that you smoke a pipe. Do you remember lighting the thing up, Frank?"

"I remember, all right," said Frank. "You made me put it out just after I got it lit."

"Yeah, well, you're too young to be smoking. Anyway, I got to thinking about it and figured what the hell. Any man my age ought to do whatever he wants to. You know what I mean, Frank? Hell, there ain't no way I could live long enough to get cancer, and I sure as hell don't have to worry about stunting my growth. I'm so old even my fingernails don't grow anymore."

"I thought you told me that it bothered your breathing," said Frank.

Warren glanced at Frank. "It does, damn it!" he snapped. "And don't you forget it! Just because I took up the habit doesn't give you the right to fire up!"

Frank said nothing. He turned to Irma with a blank look. She snarled at her husband and slowly shook her head.

"Frank, come over here and see if I'm doing this right," barked the old man.

Frank walked over to the table and picked up the pipe. "You packed it too tight," said Frank fingering the bowl.

"Too tight! What do you mean too tight? Hell, the more you pack in there, the longer it will last!" he shouted and snatched the pipe from Frank's hands. Warren struck a match and held it over the bowl of the pipe, inhaling deeply to ignite the tobacco.

"Something must be wrong with this thing," said Warren. "I'm getting light-headed just trying to draw air through the thing."

"You put too much tobacco in the thing," said Frank.

"Now, you tell me!" shouted Warren shaking the spent match. He began to suck profusely on the pipe.

"There we go. It's working now," he said proudly. By now, the kitchen was nearly filled with smoke. A bright red glow emanated from the bowl of the pipe. "I don't get it, Frank. I can hardly taste anything. What's the big deal with smoking?"

"You're not doing it right, Warren. You're supposed to inhale the smoke. Breathe it into your lungs."

Warren took a long draw from the pipe, sucking it deep within his lungs. He retched violently, spit and smoke spewing from his mouth. The coughing and gagging continued for several minutes. The old man finally regained control and then wiped his face with his handkerchief.

"That sure is good shit," he said setting the pipe on the table.

"I think you need a little more practice," said Frank.

The old man pushed the pipe further away and looked at Frank. "How's your dad doing?" he asked clearing his throat.

Frank glanced at Irma and then back at Warren. "Dad died a couple weeks ago," he said.

"What did you say?" asked Warren. "Did you say that your dad passed on?"

"I'm afraid so, Warren."

Warren stared at Frank for a few moments as if he couldn't believe what he had heard. He, then, dropped his head and began to fumble with his pipe.

"Sorry," he mumbled.

For several moments, no one spoke. Frank shuffled his feet while Warren played with his pipe.

"Well, let's get going," said Pepper walking towards the door.

"Hold on there, you two," barked Warren.

"I expect you to have that young lady home by midnight!"

"What?" asked Frank.

"You heard me. Proper young ladies need to be home at a decent hour, and midnight is late enough."

Irma started across the kitchen. "You young folks get out of here," she said. "I'll deal with this old fool."

෮ ෮ ෮

Frank pulled into the parking lot in front of the restaurant close to six. It was a small parking lot with only a few spaces, and as usual, they were all taken. He drove around the block and found a place to park on a side road nearby. He climbed out of the truck and walked around to the other side to help Pepper.

"I feel like a T-bone steak tonight," he said taking her hand.

"Of course, you know that you'd be better off with a salad instead."

"I'm sure you're right, but a steak would taste better."

The restaurant was nearly a block away, but it was a warm summer evening just right for a short stroll.

They were halfway down the street when Frank heard a door slam. Across the street was the Knight's Inn motel. Frank glanced across the street and came to an abrupt stop.

"What's the matter, Frank?" asked Pepper. He said nothing. "Are you all right?" she asked.

She, then, looked across the street in the direction he was staring. "Isn't that your son?" she asked. He still said nothing. She looked closer. "That is your son, Frank. I'm sure of it." She squinted and leaned forward. "Oh, my. Who is that with him?"

"Let's go," he said and pulled on her hand with his.

It was a nice restaurant and had been Frank's favorite for most of his life. He and Ida had celebrated every anniversary at this place since he could remember. Once inside, they were led to a large curved booth.

"Did I see what I thought I saw?" asked Pepper opening a menu.

"You saw it, all right," said Frank. "I just wish I hadn't seen it. Let's just forget it and order. What do you say?"

"Fine with me, but this should be easy. Your idea of having steak sounds good to me."

"Funny. I seem to have lost my appetite," said Frank closing his menu.

Suddenly, there was a figure standing next to their table. Frank turned and looked up. "Hi, Pop," said his son, Lloyd. "May I sit down for a moment?"

Frank said nothing. He slid around to the other side of the table next to Pepper. Lloyd sat down and folded his hands on the table in front of him.

"I'm sorry, Pop," he said in a soft voice. "Sorry you had to see that."

"Don't worry about me and what I saw. I'm a big boy. I'll get over it in time. What I want to know is if you're sorry that you did it." Lloyd said nothing. He stared at his hands resting on the table. "Well, are you?"

"Dad, you know what Helen is like, and I'm sure you can see that she's getting worse."

"Is that an excuse to go screw someone else?"

"It's not like that, Dad. It's not just a physical thing."

"And I suppose you're going to tell me that you two are in love."

"That's exactly what I'm saying. You know, Pop, we all can't be as perfect as you," said Lloyd loudly.

"Well, in all the years that I was married to your mother, I never once took another woman to bed!" Frank shouted.

"You probably didn't have to go year after year after year without sex either!" shouted Lloyd. Tables of people fell quiet as they stared at their booth. Lloyd glanced around the room and settled back into his seat. "All I'm saying is that I am a man, and I have needs. Unfortunately, Helen doesn't take care of these needs, and the worst part is she doesn't care. She just doesn't care, Dad. Hell, if the truth be known, she probably knows about this and figures what the hell."

"Why don't you get some professional help, son. I really think you two need to talk with a counselor."

"I tried that, Dad. She went to one session and declared the man incompetent. She swears she knows more than he does, and she never finished high school."

"How long have you been seeing this other woman?"

"Just over two years."

"Two years? You've been sneaking around having an affair for over two years?"

"That's right, Dad. I've been having an affair for two glorious years. For the first time in my life, I know what it's like to make love with a real woman," he said in a stern but hushed voice. "Helen thinks of sex as messy and icky. The few times that we did the deed, she would stare at the clock. I always knew why. She was afraid that she would miss the beginning of her favorite television show. Talk about a kick in your ego. No wonder there are so many guys who need a pill to get it up. They probably wouldn't need such a thing if they had a woman who would treat them like a man."

"Son, I don't have all the answers. Hell, I don't even know what most of the questions are, but I do know that what you're doing is wrong. You need professional help. Try a different counselor."

"She won't go."

"Make her go."

"Are you kidding, Dad? You've seen her in action. Do you really think she would do something that I told her to do?"

"Jesus, son. Be a man!"

"Be a man? Dad, she took my manhood away when we got married."

"Take it back, for Christ's sakes!" Frank shouted.

Pepper laid a hand on Frank's arm. "Frank, I know this is a very important discussion you and your son are having, but I'm afraid that if you keep it up, you're going to be on the six o'clock news," she said glancing around the restaurant.

Frank glanced around the room as well. "You're right," he said. "We are quite the center of attention."

"Just my luck," said Lloyd. "I wonder if I should take a bow right about now."

"Son, let me tell you one little story, and I won't say another word about it. Years ago, when you were just a kid, I had to go into town for supplies one day, and I ran into an old friend. Well, this old friend and I had dated long before I married your mother, and here we are face-to-face once again. At first, it was just normal conversation between two people who hadn't seen each other in years, but the talk soon changed. All of a sudden, she's flirting with me, and I'm flirting with her. It just happened. To this day, I'm not quite sure how, but it did. Next thing I know, she's inviting me up to her place, and I can't get rid of a big silly grin."

"I can't believe I'm hearing this," said Lloyd.

"Before I know it, I'm walking beside her, talking a mile a minute with my head stuck up her ass or mine, I'm not sure which. Suddenly, I'm staring at her as she stands there holding her door open and inviting me in."

"It scares me to ask this question, but what did you do next?"

"Son, I'm sure you know by now that there are times in every man's life when lines get drawn. Lines that you can choose to cross or choose not to. Sometimes, right and wrong get a little mixed-up. Sometimes, the lines are blurred by instinctive reaction rather than intuitive reasoning."

"In other words, you went to bed with her."

"No sir. Not on your life. I made my apologies and raced home to your mother, but here's the point I wanted to make. Your mother knew. Don't ask me how, but she knew. I had gone to town a million times before that day, and she never said a word. But not that day. She asked me so many questions I thought I was on trial.

So, don't kid yourself. Women know. They have some special sense for that kind of thing. If you've been having an affair for two years, Helen knows."

Silence fell on the table. Lloyd glanced around the room and found that people were no longer staring.

"Well, I've bothered you long enough," he said getting to his feet.

"What are you going to do, son?"

Lloyd sighed. "I don't know, Pop. I just don't know."

"I think you know your options, don't you, son?"

"Yes, and what I'm doing right now is not one of them. Right, Pop?"

"Only you know the answer to that question."

"Guess I'd better get going," said Lloyd. He took two steps, turned, and smiled at his father. "Don't want the little lady to start worrying about what I'm doing or anything."

ဢ ဢ ဢ

It was just after nine in the morning when Frank's truck pulled into Hainey's driveway. He remained in the vehicle with the motor running for a few moments until the back door opened and Pepper appeared.

"Good morning, Mr. Watson," she said as she climbed into the cab of the truck. "Now, where are you taking me on such a beautiful Sunday morning?"

"I need to go see a friend over in Jefferson County," said Frank. "He should be able to give me some information about these egg people. Do you mind coming along?"

"Not at all," she said. "It should be fun."

The trip took over two hours which included getting lost on country back roads. Finally, Frank stopped beside a mailbox in front of a farmhouse. "Howard Bower," Frank read from the nameplate attached to the mailbox. "This be the place." He pulled into the driveway and parked near the garage.

It was a simple farm with a barn and a few out buildings, all needing repairs. "Well, you can tell that the old man rules the roost at this farm," said Frank climbing out of the truck.

"How do you figure that?" asked Pepper.

"The barn's bigger than the house."

Pepper studied the barn and then turned to the house. "Okay, so the barn is bigger than the house. What does that have to do with anything?"

"There's an old saying that if the barn is bigger than the house, the man wears the pants in the family. If the house is bigger, the woman is boss."

"There's no question about it," said Pepper closing the door of the truck behind her. "The house should always be bigger. That's just the way it's supposed to be."

"No, it's not," said Frank walking around to the other side of the truck. "That doesn't even make sense. You need a big barn for the livestock, machinery, and hay. Why in the world would you need a house to be bigger than a barn, for Christ's sakes?"

The whirl of a lawnmower became louder as a gray-haired man appeared from the side of the house pushing the machine through the tall grass.

"And I suppose those stinky old hogs or whatever should get a bigger place than the people who live there. Is that what you're saying?" she asked as they began to walk towards the man who, by now, had turned off the mower.

"Frank Watson, my old friend," he said extending his hand. "What brings you to my neck of the woods?"

"Howard, you old son of a gun," said Frank taking his hand. "I want you to meet Pepper. Pepper, this is Howard."

"Nice to meet you, Howard."

"My, you're much too pretty for this old geezer. Tell me you just bummed a ride with him or something."

"Tell me something, Howard," said Pepper. "Your barn is bigger than the house. Is that why you bought the farm?"

"I got a good deal on the place," said Howard. "That's why I bought it."

"But your barn is bigger than your house. Are you all right with that?"

"Oh, no," said Howard. "If I had my way about it, the house would be bigger. Humanity is always much more important than livestock."

"Damn it, Howard," said Frank. "You're so full of shit. You're saying that just to impress the little lady here."

"Frank, just admit it," said Pepper. "You belong to another century, which one, I'm not sure."

"Frank, what brings you all the way over here," said Howard. "I'd like to think you came all this way to see me, but I'll bet there's more to it than that."

"Howard, I understand you folks around here have one of those egg factories not too far from here. What can you tell me about it?"

Howard bent over and began to clean the grass from his lawnmower. "Can't tell you a thing," he muttered.

"What do you mean you can't tell me a thing? Someone said you were unhappy with these people. I want to know why."

"What makes the difference, Frank. It's progress. That's all. It means more money coming in."

"Come on, Howard, tell me the truth. They're trying to get one of those factories over near Springfield, and I've been fighting it. I know there has to be problems when you put seven million chickens in that small of an area."

"Seven million! Is that what they told you? Try eighteen million chickens! Do you have any idea what happens when you have that many chickens in such a confined area?"

"That's why I'm here, Howard. I came to find out."

Howard leaned over again and grabbed the starting rope. "Well, you're going to have to find out from someone else," he said and pulled on the rope. The small engine came to life, and he began to push the mower over the uncut grass.

Frank walked beside the man as he finished cutting his grass. "What's the matter with you, Howard? I never saw you run scared from anyone."

Howard stopped and turned to Frank. "You don't know these people, Frank. They are scary people. They come to town and sweet talk everyone into thinking this is the right thing to do. Then, when you find out all the problems they never told us about, it's too late."

"What kind of problems?" asked Pepper.

"I can't talk about it," said Howard as he began to push the mower again.

"Come on, Howard," said Frank grabbing him by the arm. "This is your old friend, Frank. Talk to me."

Howard stopped the mower again and turned to Frank. "Well, you didn't hear this from me, but one of the many problems is the manure. Think about it. You got eighteen million chickens shittin' up a storm. Just dealing with the disposal of all that manure is more than they can handle. They spread most of it over farmlands as fertilizer. They tell you that they only spread one ton of it per acre, but we know for a fact they are spreading it at a rate of ten tons for each acre. Think about what that will do to our water supply in the near future."

"Why doesn't someone talk to them?"

"Frank, I'm sorry you came all this way for nothing, but I have to get back to work," said Howard pushing the mower again.

"Howard, you can't..."

"Got to go," he said with a wave of his hand.

Frank stared at the man until he disappeared around the side of the house. He turned and started for the truck. "Can you believe that guy? He blew me off like I was a traveling salesman or something."

"He's scared, Frank," said Pepper getting into the truck. "I think these egg people have him spooked."

"You might be right," said Frank as he climbed into the driver's seat. "Seems funny. There was a time when nothing or nobody scared Howard Bower. In fact, when we were little, Howard was the class bully. Every school has one. Howard was ours."

"I didn't see anyone else around. Is he married?"

"Oh, yeah. He's married, all right. He met a bigger bully than he ever was. He always said that's why he married her. She bullied him into it."

"Do you think he's happily married?"

"I think the jury's out on that one," said Frank pulling out onto the main road. "You see, he's been having an affair with the same woman for the last ten years."

Pepper turned to Frank. "He told you that he's been having an affair?"

"He doesn't even know that I know."

"Then, how did you find out?"

"You're kind of nosy, aren't you?"

"How did you find out?"

"Can't tell you."

"You know the woman, don't you?"

"You're prying into matters that you don't belong."

"She must be a good friend if she would tell you something as private as that."

"You know, the female brain is a work of art. You can't operate a VCR even with the instructions, but when it comes to who's screwing who..."

"Oh, my God!" she exclaimed covering her mouth with her hand. "It's Toad, isn't it?"

"If I ever need to hire a detective, I know who to go to."

"I can't believe it. All those years, he's been driving over here to see her. He must really love her."

"They had a thing when they were kids. I guess it never really died out."

"And Howard's wife doesn't know?"

"Oh, my God," said Frank. "If that day should ever come, we'll know about it the instant it happens. She's one tough woman."

"She'd do to him what I'd do to you if ever I caught you messing around behind my back."

"Think you're pretty tough, do you?"

"Tough enough to kick your butt, Mr. Watson."

"How 'bout I just not give you any reason for kicking my ass," he said as he leaned over and kissed her on the cheek.

"That suits me just fine," she said as she slid across the seat next to Frank.

11 THE ARGUMENT

The next day dawned with a fiery, orange sky. The early morning breeze was warm and dry, and this day promised to be another hot one.

Weeks had passed since Frank had first expressed opposition to the egg factory. His overt defiance had caused great concern for many of the residents of Springfield. Most of his friends were upset with him and wouldn't speak to him, while others simply avoided him.

He opened the heavy, oak door and let it close behind him. Silence fell on the room as he walked past the table of men. He walked behind the counter at the back of the room and poured himself a cup of coffee.

"Mornin', Rackets," said Frank.

"Good morning, Frank. You know if you get any more popular in this town, they'll tar and feather you."

"You know, Rackets, I didn't even think about you. My coming here every day has to be bad for your business. You say the word and I'll stay out of here until this thing blows over."

"Bullshit, Frank. Don't give it another thought. You're welcome in my restaurant anytime."

"Well, thanks, Rackets," he said. "It's nice to know I still have at least one friend."

"Oh, I didn't say anything about being your friend. In fact, I hope nobody saw me talking to you. I just need the business."

Frank paused and stared at Rackets. "Nice talking to you," he said shaking his head and walking away.

"Hi, Frank," said George.

"Good morning, George," said Frank taking a seat next to his friend.

"It's amazing the affect you have on people when you enter a room," said George.

"Kind of like Moses parting the Red Sea. Let's face it, George, I'm a shaker, a mover. I've got my finger on the pulse of America."

"I don't know about all that, Frank, but I do know that the kind people of Springfield are about to cut off all your fingers and anything else you have hanging out there."

"They love me, George," said Frank. "My people love me."

"They love you so much they're going to have a town meeting to discuss the egg factory, and guess what? You're invited. In fact, you're the main attraction."

"When is it supposed to be?"

"I don't know. I only heard bits and pieces, but I think Willard is going to give you a personal invitation."

"Good morning, Frank," said Pepper as she set a plate of food in front of him.

"Mornin', Beautiful," he said. "Damn. I don't even wait any more. You know when I'll be here and what I'll want. What if I wanted pancakes this morning?"

"It doesn't really matter," she said. "You'll eat what I bring you. It's as simple as that."

"God, do you ever sound married," said George.

"Don't you hate a woman who knows you that well?" asked Frank.

George paused as he took a sip from his coffee cup. He suddenly slammed the cup on the table. "Good God, Frank, I almost forgot. Guess who has a date tonight."

"Let me see, now," said Frank rubbing his chin. "You're taking out Pamela Anderson."

"Nope."

"Sophia Loren?"

"Not her, either."

"Raquel Welch?"

"You'll never guess."

"Then, who is it?"

"Clara Butts."

"Clara Butts? You're taking out Clara Butts? Good Grief, George. Why?"

"Do I need a reason?"

"Well, George, let's put it this way. You're not a bad looking guy. I'm sure you could do better than Clara Butts."

"Why? What's wrong with Clara?"

"Well, nothing, George. Not really. After all, beauty is only skin deep and in the eye of the beholder and all that stuff."

"You think she's fat and ugly, don't you?"

"George, what makes the difference what I think? As long as you're happy. Besides, I'm sure she has a nice personality."

"I hear she's a bitch."

"George, excuse me for asking, but why the hell are you taking her out?"

"She's a damn good cook. Hey, how do you think she got that big? Besides, she's got big tits."

"George, tits is such a vulgar word to use. Cows have tits. Women have breasts."

"Since when did you get so sensitive? Have you been reading one of those women's magazines?"

"And they say I'm backwards. Old Frank belongs to another century. Completely out of touch. At least, I don't refer to women's breasts as tits."

"It's in the dictionary, you know."

"What's in the dictionary?"

"Tits. It's in the dictionary. I looked it up."

"I'm sure it is, George. Now, will you drop it? I'm beginning to feel like we're back in school."

George drank from his coffee cup and pushed his empty plate away. "I still don't know why you have to be so sensitive about a word that's in the dictionary," he muttered aloud.

"Excuse me, Frank," came a loud voice from the other end of the table. Frank looked up to see Willard Miller staring at him from the end table. "I wonder if I might have a moment of your time?"

"As always, Willard, you've got the floor."

"Frank, there's going to be town meeting over at the schoolhouse next Tuesday night. Do you think you might be able to attend?"

"Wouldn't miss it for the world," said Frank. "I hope we're going to talk about when we're going to get the new sewer system. George's septic tank is getting full again, and I don't want to help him empty it."

There was muffled laughter up and down the table. "You know why we're meeting, Frank," said Willard. "It's to discuss the chickens and the egg business."

"All the more reason to get on with the sewer system," said Frank. "That many chickens using the toilets of Springfield will fill up the septic tanks in no time."

More laughter from the table. All eyes turned to Willard. "Have your little joke, Frank," said Willard. "Come July the fifth, though, we'll put an end to this issue once and for all."

"You know, Willard, the rumor is that you've been impotent for the last six months, and it just seems like that the longer you go without getting laid, the grumpier you get."

"Never mind about that shit," said Willard. "Just be there Tuesday night."

Glances were exchanged, and low muttering began around the table.

"Jesus, Frank," said George. "Don't you think you should go easy on Willard? Half the town wants to lynch you Tuesday night, and you're just stirring the stick in the pot."

"Let me tell you something, George. These people are dishonest. I know it as well as I know anything. I know they had something to do with Merle's death, and I know that this chicken farm will mean major problems for this town."

"Did you ever talk with Howard Bower?"

"He ain't saying a word. He's scared of these people. In fact, he's smarter than we are. At least, he knows enough to be scared."

"That's too bad," said George. "You really could use him next Tuesday. It would help if he was here."

"By the way, George, where are you taking Clara on your date?" he asked pulling money from his pocket.

"I thought I'd take her over to the Star Lanes in Marion to go bowling."

"Bowling! Women don't want to go bowling on their first date. They want to go somewhere romantic like dinner at a fancy restaurant and then to a movie or dancing, but not bowling. Whatever made you decide to take her bowling?"

"Clara likes the way they fry the onions up before they put 'em on her hamburger."

Frank dropped a five-dollar bill onto the table. "Sounds like you're in for a romantic evening," he said. "Tell 'em to put extra onions on to be sure." He winked at Pepper, turned, and walked out of the restaurant.

ဆ ဆ ဆ

It was early afternoon when Frank stepped outside the back door. He had errands to do in town, so he cut across the backyard in the direction of his truck. He just reached it when a black automobile turned into the drive. It came to a stop just behind where his truck was parked, and four men dressed in suits got out.

"Good afternoon, Mr. Watson," said one of the men. "Do you remember me?"

"You're from the egg factory," said Frank. "Ballinger is your name, I believe."

"I'm impressed, Mr. Watson. You have a good memory."

"You're hardly the kind of people I would soon forget."

"Mr. Watson, I promised to send you an offer on your farm quite some time ago. I hope you don't mind, but I'm bringing it to you myself," said Ballinger extending an envelope in Frank's direction.

"Not interested," said Frank staring at the sealed envelope.

"Mr. Watson, I think you'll find that it's a very generous offer.

"Doesn't matter. I'm not interested."

Mr. Watson, we're moving into your town, one way or the other. Wise up, Frank. Why shouldn't you get in on the ground floor and make some money for yourself?"

Frank turned to face Ballinger. "Look, I know you think of me as some dumb farmer. Some boob who couldn't pour piss from a boot even with the instructions. Well, let me tell you something. I can't prove it, but I know you're dirty. I know you tampered with my brakes, and I know you had something to do with Merle Henson's death."

"Those are pretty serious allegations, Mr. Watson. I hope you prepared to back that up."

"I don't have to back up shit," said Frank turning towards his truck.

"Are you coming to the town meeting next Tuesday?"

"Wouldn't miss it for anything."

"Really, Mr. Watson? I am surprised. I'm sure you're smart enough to know that you don't have a chance. Hell, Custer had better odds," he said with a smirk.

Frank opened the door of his truck. "You know, son," said Frank with a smile. "There's an old saying about lawyers. It goes something like 99 per cent of lawyers give the rest a bad name. I'm sure that saying could be applied to whatever line of work you're in," he said as he climbed into the cab of his truck. "Now, if you wouldn't mind moving that hearse of yours. I need to get out."

The four men did not move. Frank leaned his head out the window. "Did you happen to notice that big piece of lumber on the back of my truck where the bumper used to be? If you don't move your car, I will."

The men glanced at one another and then scrambled into the car. Seconds later, Frank had clearance to back out of his drive.

⇛ ⇛ ⇛

The rest of the week went by quickly, and Frank became more uneasy as each day passed. He met with disdain from everyone he encountered. Even George, his best friend, seemed distant.

It was early Friday evening, and Frank found himself pacing the kitchen floor. Pepper had called and was on her way over. Frank had tried to dissuade her from coming. It wasn't that he didn't love her and enjoy her company. In fact, that was quite the contrary. It was just that he needed this time to sort his thoughts and prepare for the town meeting.

Frank wandered into the living room and sat in Ida's favorite chair. His eyes scanned the living room walls, his mind escaping to a time long ago. For a moment, his hands relaxed on the arm of the chair.

"It stood in that corner that year," muttered Frank pointing at a spot on the other side of the room. "I couldn't understand why Pop put it in that corner that particular year. It seemed so strange. It had always gone over there near the fireplace. I thought Pop had gone crazy. Do you know what I mean, Ida? Some things are just not supposed to change, and that's one of them. The Christmas tree should be in the same place every year."

Frank stared into the memories of years gone by, of an era that would never again be. He shifted his weight in the chair; his eyes remained fixed and unblinking. "You know, Ida, it was years later when I made the connection. I couldn't understand why he put the tree in that corner, and even after that Christmas was over, I didn't put two and two together. Pop had bought me a brand-new bicycle, a 26-inch Schwinn with the tank and everything. That's why he put the tree over there. He needed the room to put the bike next to the tree. God, what a Christmas that was. I remember running down the stairs and finding that absolutely beautiful bicycle. I don't think I ever was as excited or happy as that one moment in my life."

Frank turned his head in the direction of the barn. "I still have 'er, Ida. She's hanging from the rafters in the barn. Ain't that something, Ida? After all those years, I still own that wonderful bicycle that used to take me away...away from it all. Just me and my bike and the wind in my hair. God, I miss that bike."

It was seven o'clock, and the clock on the mantel began to chime. Frank shook his head and rubbed his face with his hand. His eyes scanned the room. He frowned and settled back in his chair. "You're not here, are you?" he asked aloud. "Doesn't that figure? When I need you the most, you leave me? The whole world has turned its back on me, and I can't even count on you."

Frank got to his feet and began to pace. "My God, what am I going to do?" he muttered. He continued to pace for several moments until suddenly he stopped in the middle of the living room. He turned and gazed out the window at the field of wheat. "Take me back, dear God. Just one more time, let me run down the stairs. Just one more time. Let me smell the sweetness of Christmas one more time. Let me feel my mother's touch and know that safe feeling wrapped inside my father's arms. Dear God, help me. I beg you. I need your help."

Suddenly, the quiet was shattered by the loud report of the back door closing.

"Hello, Frank!" shouted Pepper. "Where are you?"

Frank stepped into the kitchen. "Hi, Pepper," he said kissing her on the cheek.

"Are you all right?" she asked staring into his eyes.

"I'm fine," he said walking over to the window.

"You're worried about the town meeting, aren't you?"

"I'm going to need a miracle."

"You need Howard Bower and his friends from Jefferson County to be there Tuesday night. That's what you need."

"You know, this has been difficult for me, make no mistake about it. But you know the toughest part of it all? These are all my friends. These people who won't speak to me anymore have been friends of mine all my life. That's the part I can't take."

"I'm still your friend," said Pepper sitting down on one of the chairs. Frank said nothing. He stared out the window. "Sit down, Frank," she said. The man remained motionless. "Come on, Frank. Please sit down. I have something I want to discuss with you."

He turned and stared at her for a moment and then slowly pulled out a chair to sit down.

"Frank, I know you've got a lot on your mind, but I have to ask you something."

"What is it?" he asked.

She reached across the table and took one of his weathered hands into hers. "Frank, I just need to know how you feel about me. We talk and spend time together, but we never really talk about us. Do you know what I mean, Frank?"

Frank pulled back his hand and dropped into his lap. "You know how I feel about you."

"No, I don't, Frank," she said leaning over the table. "I know you've told me that you love me. I can't exactly remember when it was, but I'm sure that it happened. I guess I just need to hear it again. That's all."

Frank gave her a puzzled look. "Well, if that's all you want. Sure thing. I love you."

"You don't get it, do you? I'm asking you to share with me your feelings. I'm not asking for your hat size, Frank."

"Jesus, Pepper. You know that I love you. There's never been any question of that."

"Yes, there has been a question. I never hear you say it, Frank. A girl needs to hear it more than once a month."

"All right! All right! I'll try to do better. I'll try to tell you that I love you more often. Okay?"

Pepper paused as she stared at the man sitting across the table. "Frank, I'm sure that you love me, but what's going to happen to us? Where are we going with this relationship?"

Frank sat back in his chair and moved it away from the table. "Oh, for Christ's sakes, Pepper! Do we have to do this right now?"

"Yes, Frank," she said sternly. "We have to do this right now."

"Why?"

"I have my reasons."

"You have incredible timing, woman."

"Don't call me that!"

"Don't call you what?"

"Don't call me woman like that. I don't like to be called that in that tone of voice."

Frank got to his feet. "Jesus Christ, Pepper! Did you just come over here to fight or what?"

"Actually, I came over here to get some answers to some questions, and like it or not, I'm getting my answers!"

"What the hell does that mean?"

"It means that there is no sensitive side to you. It means you can't share your feelings. That's what it means."

"Christ, Pepper. I have the whole town about to string me up, and you have to hit me with this!"

Pepper leaned back in her chair. "Goddamn, Frank! All I wanted to know was if there was a future for you and me! That's all! I think I have a right to know!"

"Well, you're not getting an answer right now, Pepper!" shouted Frank. "I don't know what's going to happen to you and me. I just can't deal with it right now."

Pepper got to her feet and started for the door. "Trust me!" she shouted with one hand on the doorknob. "You won't have to deal with it! I'll make sure of that! I have better things to do with my time!" With that, she stormed out the door and slammed it behind her.

12 THE FOURTH OF JULY

It was late morning on the Fourth of July, and the sun was already high in the sky. Frank started the grill and closed the lid. For the first time, Frank was sorry that his children were coming over to the house. With all that was happening in his life, he was having a difficult time relaxing.

The impending town meeting was a great concern to him, but his real problem was Pepper. For the past two days, Frank had called everyone trying to find her. Rackets had given her the weekend off and, the restaurant was closed on the holiday. Irma Hainey said that she had packed a bag and left Friday night. Neither her nor Warren had heard from her on Saturday or Sunday.

Frank was feeling guilty about Pepper's leaving town. He was sure that it was because of the fight they had on Friday night. It seemed so pointless and avoidable. He knew she was upset, but he didn't think she would go this far.

Just as Frank opened the grill to check the fire, an expensive-looking black sedan pulled into the driveway and parked in front of the sidewalk. Fear struck Frank. The car looked like the same one owned by the egg factory people. It was bad enough that these intimidating people came to his house when he was there. He certainly didn't want them to stop when his family was there.

Frank started towards the automobile. He was halfway there when the driver's door opened and a tall, young man dressed in a suit got out of the car. Frank stopped and studied the man. He didn't look familiar. The egg people had been to his house several times, and Frank did not recognize this man as being one of them.

Just then, the passenger side door opened, and a woman got out of the car. She had her back to him, and Frank could not identify her. She, then, turned and waved at Frank. "Hi, Dad," she said.

Frank sighed relief as he recognized his daughter, Betty. "Hello, there," he shouted with a smile.

"How are you, Pop?" she asked as she fell into his arms.

"I'm fine. How are you?"

"How did you use to put it? I'm on top of the world!" she shouted. "I want to introduce to you the reason why. Dad, this is my friend, Marcus."

"Glad to meet you, Mr. Watson," he said extending a hand.

"Nice meeting you," said Frank shaking his hand.

"Marcus is a lawyer," said Betty. "We met for the first time twenty-two days and three hours ago. We were in court arguing a case against each other."

"Who won?" asked Frank.

"I did," said Betty.

"No, you didn't," said Marcus. "The judge hasn't made his final ruling."

"But you know he's going to rule in my favor."

Frank gently grabbed the young man's arm. "Save yourself some aggravation and let her have her way. Her mother was the most stubborn woman I ever knew, and her daughter inherited every bit of it."

The three people began to slowly walk towards the house. "Dad, I heard about the town meeting tomorrow night. Are you going to be all right?"

"Oh, don't you worry about me," he said. "It'll take more than this bunch of yahoos to get the best of me."

"Well, from what I hear, the meeting is just a nice word for a lynching. It sounds to me like they're going to gang up on you."

"You know what really bothers me is that I thought this was America where you had the freedom of choice. I thought that in America you could choose where you want to live and for how long. Ain't it funny what happens to people when the almighty dollar enters into the picture?"

"Is there anything I can do? Would you like for me to go with you tomorrow night? It might not hurt to have a lawyer with you. Besides, I might even give you a break on my fee."

"Right now, the best thing you could do is to help me get this meal on the table. Your brother and his tribe of misfits will be here soon, and I don't even have the chicken on the grill."

It was nearly noon when an older model station wagon pulled into the driveway. The vehicle stopped just behind the other cars, and the driver reached up and turned off the engine.

Frank strained to see inside the car. He could see his son and his wife in the front seat and their two sons in the back. Several moments passed. Frank took several steps closer and bent over to see better. He could see that Lloyd was talking. By his arm gestures and the movement of his head, it appeared that he was giving instructions to both Helen and the boys.

Finally, all four doors opened at once, and they all got out of the vehicle and started for the house.

"Hi, Pop," he said waving his hand. "Hi, Sis."

The two young boys slowly walked over to where Frank was standing and stopped right in front of him. "Hi, Grandpa," they said in unison. "May we sit down at the table?"

Frank said nothing. He stared down at the two boys, his mouth open wide. The two boys remained motionless waiting for an answer. Frank turned to Betty who had a wide-eyed look of disbelief and then back to the young boys. "Sure," he muttered.

"Hi, Dad," said Helen kissing him on the cheek. "My, you're looking good. How are you, Betty?"

"I'm fine," she said giving her a quick hug.

"Is this a friend of yours?" asked Helen.

"Oh, oh, yes," said Betty. "Helen, this is my friend, Marcus."

"Glad to meet you, Marcus," she said shaking his hand. "My name is Helen, and that handsome man bringing the picnic basket is my husband."

There was silence as they all watched Lloyd walk slowly in their direction. He stopped in front of the group of people and said with a smile, "Let's eat!"

Minutes later, they were all seated at the picnic table enjoying the food. Very little was said as they finished their chicken, potato salad, and baked beans.

Frank was nearly finished when he dropped his fork on his empty plate and got to his feet. "I'll be right back," he announced to the others. "I have a fresh strawberry pie in the house made just for today." He picked up his empty plate and disappeared into the back of the house.

He had just removed the pie from the refrigerator when the back door opened and closed.

"Need any help?" came a voice from across the kitchen.

Frank turned to see his son standing just inside. "Lloyd, what's going on?" asked Frank.

"What do you mean?"

"What happened to Helen? I've never seen her like this before."

"I took 'em back."

"You took what back?"

"My gonads. I took them back, and it feels great."

"Just like that? That's all there was to it?"

"I was so ashamed of her last Memorial Day when we were here that I decided it was time for a change. Well, that night when we got home, we got into it. Boy, was that a humdinger. The fight of the century. It went on until the next morning. The bottom line was that I wasn't going to give in this time, and if she didn't go to a see a counselor with me, I was going to leave her. For once in her life, she took me seriously because we've been going ever since."

"What about that other woman you were seeing?"

"We broke it off. I knew what I was doing was wrong, but I guess it took the shock of your catching me to really wake me up."

"Well, that's fantastic, son. I can't believe the change in her. He must be a great counselor to make Helen change like that."

"It's not that he's that great of a counselor," said Lloyd. "It's the fact that he looks like Tom Cruise. She wouldn't think of missing a session."

"What about the kids? They aren't seeing this counselor, are they?"

"No, but you'd think so from the way they have changed. It's strange, but they started changing when we stopped fighting. It's funny how it all fell into place."

"Well, I'm happy for you, son. I really am. It's so nice to see you in charge again, and to see Helen treating you with the respect you deserve."

Just then, Helen's voice boomed from the backyard. "What's holding up the Goddamn pie?" she shouted. "We're out here waiting!"

Frank turned to his son, and Lloyd turned to his father. "Hey, she's not perfect!" said Lloyd with a shrug of his shoulders.

The rest of the day went by as Fourth of Julys often do. The heat of that mid-summer day was tempered with a soft and gentle breeze that seemed to soothe and caress. Adults relaxed in cushioned chairs, while children explored the farm and all the adventures that it had to offer. Distant reports from exploding fireworks served as a reminder that this was a holiday unique in origin and rich in tradition.

It was early evening when the tired old station wagon pulled out of Frank's drive and onto the road in front of his house.

"Well, I hope things work out for him," said Betty as she watched the car disappear down the road.

"What a difference!" said Frank. "Helen was almost human."

"It certainly looks as if Lloyd has his life on track now," said Betty. "Maybe, he'll be able to end his little fling with that other woman now."

Frank turned to his daughter. "Now, how the hell did you know about that?"

"Oh, I've known about that for over a year now."

"Good God!" said Frank. "How do you women do it? Nothing seems to slip by you people. Do you have some kind of radar for that kind of thing?"

"Any woman will tell you, Pop. It's a girl thing, and how we do it is a very well-kept secret."

"Damn, I can believe that!"

"Well, Dad, we need to get going. Are you sure you don't want me to go with you tomorrow night?" she asked as they walked slowly towards the car.

"I'll be fine," he said opening the car door for her. "It's just a couple of bullies in town making trouble for me. The others will come around once this thing blows over."

"Nice meeting you, Mr. Watson," said Marcus shaking his hand.

"Take care of my little girl," said Frank. "She's the only one I have."

Marcus got into the driver's side and started the engine. Moments later, the car pulled out of the drive and onto the road in front of Frank's house. Frank watched until the car was out of sight.

Suddenly, Frank had an overwhelming sense of loneliness. He walked slowly to the back yard and eased himself into his favorite chair. The wind was much stronger now and made him wince as he stared across a field of wheat. The wind rolled across the stalks of grain like waves against the shore.

The wind played with Frank's sparse hair sending it in one direction than another. A lone tear darted down his cheek. "From the earth we are formed, and so shall we return," Frank whispered aloud. "Dear God. I miss you, Ida. I need you by my side right now. I feel so alone."

A gust of wind seemed to swallow his words and carry them off. Frank lifted his head upwards and squinted at the dark gray clouds that were speeding his way. "I'm all alone, now. I know it. As sure as anything, I'm all alone. How could you leave me, Ida? How could you leave me alone?"

A fine mist of rain began to fall. The small drops hit Frank's face like pellets from a gun. Within moments, the rain hit, sending a downpour that descended in sheets of violent attack.

Still staring at the heavens, Frank slowly got to his feet and walked across the lawn to the back door of his house.

13 THE TOWN MEETING

It was the event of the year for the little town of Springfield. The last town meeting was years ago when the decision was made to put in a sewer system. Most of the town's people excitedly crowded into the gymnasium of the local high school for that one.

Tonight's meeting promised to be even a bigger hit. When the doors of the school opened at six o'clock, there was already a line of people waiting. No event had been so important since one of the two feed mills in town closed.

Within a half-hour, nearly all the seats were filled, and people were still filing in. Calvin, the school janitor, brought out a wagonload of folding metal chairs, and with the help of some friends, began to set up more rows of seats.

All the chairs were taken quickly except for a few in the front row just in front of the stage. There was a low murmuring throughout the crowd as everyone quietly discussed the egg factory. Two more people walked across the gym floor and found two chairs in the front row.

Willard Miller walked across the stage and stopped in front of the microphone. He blew into it. Nothing. He tapped on it. Still nothing. Willard scowled at Calvin who got to his feet and started for a small room at one end of the stage where the controls were kept.

Willard blew into the microphone again. This time, he could be heard echoing through the room. "Testing," he blared. "Testing. Testing." He tapped the microphone several times. "Turn it down, Calvin!" Seconds later, he tapped on it again. "There. That's better. Come on out of there, Calvin. Someone's liable to steal your seat." There was still a low murmuring of the crowd as they waited for the meeting to begin.

Suddenly, the crowd went quiet. Onto the gym floor walked Frank Watson. He stood there for several moments searching the room for a seat. The only empty chair was in the front row just in front of Willard.

A hush fell on the room as he walked to the front of the room. Willard watched intently as Frank found an empty chair and sat down. Frank crossed his legs and leaned back.

"Well, I guess we can begin," said Willard staring at Frank. "I know you're all wondering what I'm doing up here. Where's that damn mayor of ours is what you're thinking. Well, Clyde couldn't be here tonight. He sold his prize heifer yesterday. You all remember the one. It took the blue ribbon at the county fair last year. Well anyway, Clyde had to run her up to Willow Springs, and he asked me run things for him tonight. Hope y'all don't mind too much. Of course, I don't really care if you do, so with no more further jawing, let's get on with it."

The entire crowd seemed to shift in their seats as they prepared for the main event.

"We're all here tonight to discuss this egg factory business once and for all. There are a lot of people who want to get their two cents in, but you're just going to have to be patient. Half the town is here tonight, and we don't want this thing to take all night.

I think the first order of business is to have Mr. Ballinger, who represents the egg factory, come up here on stage."

A low murmur went through the crowd as a man dressed in a suit strutted across the floor. He climbed the steps that led to the stage and walked over to the microphone. The room fell silent. The man adjusted the microphone and dropped his hands to his sides. For several moments, he gazed over the crowd with a broad smile.

"Good evening, ladies and gentlemen of Springfield," he announced in a bold voice. "My name is Mike Ballinger, and I am here to bring lots of money to your town!" The crowd erupted in cheers and applause.

"That's all I want to do, folks, is bring money and prosperity to your town." More applause. "We want to give you top dollar for about five hundred acres on which to erect our small factory. That's all. You won't even know we're here. We blend right in with the community, and for the privilege of being allowed to move here, we promise to pump tons of money into your economy. After all, we're all in this together. Right?" More applause.

Ballinger stepped back from the microphone for a few moments and then returned when the crowd became quiet. "There are those who oppose our coming to your town. To them, I say God bless you. This is America, and every man has a right to his opinion. I must warn you though that this is a once in a lifetime. Opportunities like this don't come around every day. Indeed, this could be Springfield's last chance at progress and a glimpse at the future. Hell, the whole world is marching forward, folks. I just want your town to have a piece of it. That's all." He held up his arms. "Come with me, good people of Springfield. March with me into the future."

The entire room got to its feet, cheering and applauding. Ballinger stepped back from the microphone as Willard walked across the stage smiling and clapping his hands.

Within moments, the noise subsided, and Willard grabbed the microphone. "Damn! That sure was some speech! I swear for a moment there I thought I was in church. Now folks, let's open the floor. Any questions for Mr. Ballinger? Now, is the time."

The two men squinted into the dark crowd. "Hell, Calvin, go turn up the lights. I can't see a thing. The janitor got up from his chair and started for the control room again. In a moment, the lights snapped on.

"There," said Willard. "That's better. Sorry, Calvin. I ain't doing much for that corn on your foot, am I? All right, folks.

Does anyone have any questions for Mr. Ballinger while we got him here?"

A man stood in the back of the room. "Mr. Ballinger, I heard a rumor that there's a real problem with the disposal of manure."

"I'm glad you asked that question," said Ballinger. "We all know about rumors and how the truth gets lost along the way. Well, I'm here to tell you that we turned that problem into an asset. As you all know, manure is one of nature's greatest fertilizers. We have an effective collection system, and then we sell it to the farmers in the area for a rock bottom price. One hand washes the other. I think you'll find that we've done our homework, folks. Nothing has been overlooked."

"Any more questions?" asked Willard.

Another man stood. "What's in it for us? We take a chance on you people coming here. What do we get out of this?"

Ballinger grabbed the microphone and pulled it closer. "Money! That's what you get out of this. Good old American dollars. Besides bringing a substantial tax base to your community, we plan to make considerable donations to the town. After all, we would be a member of the community and a concerned citizen. Why wouldn't we want the town to prosper while we're here?"

"What kind of donations are we talking about?"

"As soon as we begin construction, I am prepared to make a ten-thousand-dollar donation, and don't forget our chickens have to eat. We plan to buy corn from the farmers in this area, and we plan to give top dollar."

Applause erupted. Several minutes passed before the room became quiet again.

"Any more questions for Mr. Ballinger?" asked Willard. Several moments passed. "Anybody?"

"What about the flies?" came a voice in the front row.

"Who asked that question?" asked Willard.

"I did," said Frank holding up his hand.

Ballinger stepped in front of Willard taking the microphone from him. "Mr. Watson, I was wondering when we would be hearing from you."

"What about the flies?"

"I'm sorry, but I didn't know there was a problem with flies."

"I was over in Jefferson County visiting a friend of mine who lives real close to your other factory, and I noticed that there were flies everywhere."

"Mr. Watson, I think that was your imagination working overtime. We take precaution against the possibility of a fly problem. We introduce the Darkling Beetle to the area. The Darkling Beetle is a harmless insect that loves fly larvae. They walk around all day eating fly larvae before they hatch. So, you see, Mr. Watson, I think you're exaggerating the problem just a little. Perhaps, the next time you visit your friend in Jefferson County, you might want to bring along a fly swatter."

The crowd remained silent. Frank said nothing more.

Willard leaned over into the microphone. "All right, folks. I think it's time we heard from Frank. Come on up here, Frank." The crowd applauded. "Come on, Frank."

Frank got up from his chair and slowly walked onto the stage. Willard and Ballinger stepped back. Frank grabbed the microphone. His hands were shaking violently, so he returned his hands to his sides.

"Hello!" he shouted into the microphone. "Wow! That's loud. Is it supposed to be that loud?"

"Just speak naturally," whispered Willard.

"What?" asked Frank.

"Step back from the mike. They can hear you."

"Oh," said Frank stepping back. He cleared his throat and stared into the crowd. Several moments passed. He bent over slightly as he studied the room from one end to the other.

"Come on, Frank," came a voice from the back. "Let's get on with it."

He thrust his hands into his pockets and stepped up to the microphone. "You folks have known me all your lives."

"Louder, Frank!" came a voice.

"You folks have known me all your lives. I've lived in this town all my life. Hell, the Watson name has been here from the beginning. I don't think in all the years I've lived here that I've slept more than three nights away from home, and that was the time when Ida and I won that trip to Las Vegas. A lot of good it did to go there. Ida wouldn't even let me play the slot machines.

Well, anyway, I've been a part of this community for a long time. I couldn't help but look out at you folks out there and notice that I don't think there's a face I don't recognize. I don't think there's a one of you out there that I haven't helped in some way or other over the last several years. If I haven't helped you combine your wheat or mend your fence, I watched your kids for you while you went to the movies. But that's all right. That's what neighbors are for. That's what friends are for. I help you. You help me. I rejoice in your successes, and you mourn with me." Frank paused for a moment. The crowd became silent. "I don't think," he started to say and then bowed his head. "I don't think there was a dry eye at Ida's funeral."

Frank did not move. There was an eerie silence throughout the room. "I guess that's the part of this thing that bothers me the most," said Frank looking out at the crowd. "Because I oppose this chicken factory, I have become an outcast of my own town. How could the all mighty dollar become more important than friendship?"

Willard stepped over to the microphone. "Frank, we just want to know why. Why are you so opposed to these fine people?"

Frank paused as he approached the microphone once again. "I know you want some kind of fancy speech from me. You want to hear some hard-core facts that will change your minds about this thing. Well, I'm sorry. All I know is that there is something unnatural about sticking that many chickens in that small of an area. It just ain't natural. Nothing good is going to come of it."

Ballinger stepped forward. "Do you have any proof, Mr. Watson? Any proof that this is detrimental to the environment or to the people who live nearby?"

Frank paused. The audience became noisy. "Not really."

"Why not, Mr. Watson. Surely you will agree that these kind people that you call your friends deserve more than just talk.

They deserve proof. In America, we don't go around making wild accusations without proof. How would you feel if we went around accusing you of some dastardly deed without proof? Did you even try to get any proof?"

"Like I said. I went over to Jefferson County to talk to some people I know."

"Okay. Where are they, Mr. Watson? We all would like to hear from them right now! We deserve to hear from them right now! Give us the proof that we need so that these good people can decide for themselves."

Frank stepped back from the microphone. He pulled his handkerchief from his back pocket and wiped the sweat from his forehead. He returned the handkerchief to his pocket and slowly walked to the microphone. The crowd was noisy and restless. "Come on, Frank!" came a voice. "Let's hear what you have to say." Frank reached for the microphone, his hand shaking profusely.

Suddenly, there was a loud crashing sound as the doors at the rear of the gymnasium burst open. The crowd grew silent as all eyes followed a procession of about twenty people boldly marching across the floor towards the stage.

Frank stared intently at the group of people coming at him. They were almost to the steps when he realized who was leading the group. "Oh, my God!" he muttered aloud. "It's Pepper!"

She marched up the stairs and stood at the center of the stage, followed by nineteen denim-clad farmers, carrying feed bags. They all huddled around Pepper as she grabbed the microphone. "Most of you people know me. For those of you who don't eat Racket's greasy food, my name is Pepper Ledley. Now, I missed the first part of this so-called meeting, but I can pretty much guess how it's been going from the faces I see around here.

I know that some of you people came here tonight to hear the truth. I know that you're all good people and deserve the truth, so I brought some people from Jefferson County with me tonight. These people have been living next to an egg factory for quite some time. Would you like to hear what they have to say?"

There was a sharp round of applause. "Without further ado, let me introduce Howard Bower. Hell, I understand he used to live around here. Howard, the stage is all yours," she said and stepped back until she was next to Frank. Frank turned and looked at her. He was still in shock. "Close your mouth, Frank. It's not that attractive." He snapped his mouth closed and turned to Howard who was stepping up to the microphone.

Howard grabbed the microphone and turned to the men behind him. "All right, gentlemen, do it!" he shouted.

All eighteen men opened the tops of the feed bags that they were holding and dumped the contents onto the stage. Dozens of rotted chicken carcasses spilled onto the floor of the stage. The crowd was repulsed as they stared at the display.

"What you see here is just part of the problem," said Howard. "What we're talking about here is eighteen million chickens in a five-hundred-acre area! They don't tell you that, folks. In fact, there are a lot of things they don't tell you. Like these dead chickens you see here. They don't tell you about that problem. Folks, they have seven hundred chickens dying every day!

That's nearly five thousand in a week! What would you do with five thousand dead chickens every week? Well, I'll tell you what they do. Those dead chickens end up with the fertilizer spread all over your fields. They tell you that they spread the manure over your fields at a rate of a ton per acre. We know for a fact that they are spreading it at a rate of ten tons per acre! Folks, what do you think that's going to do to your water supply?"

There was a low murmur through the crowd.

"How would you like to spend the rest of your lives with flies so thick that you can't even sit outdoors? And don't fall for that story about the Darkling Beetle. Hell, they're worse than the flies. That damn beetle is everywhere. They infest your homes, your kitchens, and your beds. I killed hundreds of them in my pantry alone."

Frank turned to Pepper and whispered into her ear. "How in the hell did you ever get him to do this?"

"It's called the power of a woman," she said with a smile.

"What are you talking about?"

"There are some things a woman can do that a man can't, and this was one of them."

"Okay, I'll agree with that, but what did you say to him? What could you possibly say to him to convince him to come here tonight?"

"It wasn't what I said. It was what Toad said."

"What does Toad have to do with this?"

"I asked her for some help persuading Howard to help us."

"And just what did she say to Howard to convince him to come over here tonight?"

Scott Fields

"I don't know. I wasn't there, but I think it had something to do with their relationship and what Howard's wife might say if she ever found out."

"That's blackmail!" shouted Frank.

"Is that what you call it?" asked Pepper. "I call it the power of woman."

Frank turned to Howard and back to Pepper. "Remind me to be nicer to you. You are no one to mess with," he said wrapping an arm around her.

"I promise to always remind you to be nice to me," she said with a smile.

Howard continued for over a half-hour presenting facts and answering questions. Before he was finished, Ballinger quietly walked off stage and disappeared through a back exit.

By nine o'clock, the meeting was over, and everyone returned to their homes.

ℰℰℰ

It was just after seven o'clock the next morning when Frank stopped in front of Wilton's Garage. He slid across the seat and climbed out the passenger side of the vehicle.

"Sam!" he shouted. "Where the hell are you?"

From inside the building, he could hear a voice. "Who the hell is making all the noise?" Sam Wilton appeared wiping his hands with a rag. "Well, I'll be. If it ain't Frank Watson. Do you have any idea what a hero you are in this town?"

"Never mind that shit!" barked Frank. "That door on the truck that you fixed. Do you remember that?"

"Yeah."

"Well, it doesn't work anymore. I want my money back."

"I didn't charge you in the first place."

"Well, fix it then! For Christ's sakes, Sam, I have a girlfriend now. I don't think it will impress her none if the door on my truck doesn't work."

"Oh, I'm sure that will make a difference, Frank. So, what you're saying is that she'll be impressed with that old turd if the doors work?"

"Hey! She's impressed with this old turd! Don't give me a hard time! Just fix the damn thing before I get back from breakfast!" Frank shouted. He turned and began to walk away.

"Nice talking to you, as always, Frank!" shouted Sam.

It was a beautiful summer morning, and Frank enjoyed the walk across town to the diner.

He pulled open the front door and let it close behind him. A chorus of voices went up as he entered the room. Many cheered, and others clapped.

Frank walked to the back of the restaurant to pour himself a cup of coffee.

Rackets stepped up beside him to put the till into the register. "Hey, everyone else deserted you, Frank, but remember who remained your friend."

Frank looked at the big man with a puzzled look. "I thought you told me you just needed the business."

"I did," said Rackets. "But that's kind of like being your friend."

Frank stared at the man for a moment and then walked over to the table.

"Hey, Frank!" shouted Ben Sager. "Did you hear what happened to that Ballinger fellow and his friends? They arrested him for murder. I guess they got enough evidence on them for Merle Hensen's death."

Frank sat down next to George with a stunned look on his face.

"Hey, Frank! Any chance you'd be willing to run for mayor? I don't think there's a soul in town who wouldn't vote for you."

Willard was sitting at the end of the table. He looked at Frank and smiled. "Hell, even I'd vote for you, Frank," he said, and everyone began to laugh.

"These people are easily impressed," said Frank taking a sip of coffee.

"Shit, Frank!" said George. "Right now, there ain't a man in Springfield who wouldn't give you his life savings that's buried in his backyard if you asked. There ain't a woman who wouldn't drop to her knees if you asked her. You're a goddamn hero, Frank."

"George, today is a special day, and it isn't because of last night."

"What are you talking about?"

"I'll show you in a minute," he said getting to his feet.

"What the hell are you doing?" asked George.

Pepper was working her way down the table taking orders for breakfast from the men. As she finished with each one, she proceeded down the table until she came to George.

"George, what can I get for you?"

George looked up at Frank who was still standing next to him. "I'll have the usual. Over easy, this time, though," he said.

The restaurant became silent as she turned to Frank. "And what can I get for you, Mr. Watson?" she asked with a smile.

Frank grabbed his chin and looked at the ceiling. "Let me see," he said slowly. "I believe I'll have something different this morning. I believe I'll ask you for your hand in marriage. Miss Ledley, would you marry me?"

All eyes turned towards the couple standing in the middle of the room.

Pepper grabbed her chin and stared at the ceiling. "You know something, Mr. Watson?" she asked. "That works out about right since your next child could sure use a daddy."

Frank's mouth dropped open. "Do you mean to tell me..."

"I tried to tell you last Friday night, but you were so darn worried about the meeting."

"I'm going to be a father?"

"And a husband," she added.

Frank wrapped her in his arms and gave her a long and passionate kiss with the sound of applause in the background.

Sam fixed that door on the truck, and it never was a problem again.

A month later, Frank traded it in for a new one. He was heard to say that its time had finally come.

THE END

SCOTT FIELDS
THE AUTHOR

In 1966, Scott turned down a contract with the Detroit Tigers to pursue his lifelong dream of becoming a published author by earning a degree at Ohio University. In 1996 with a lifelong dream of being a writer, Scott started writing short stories. Within two years, he had four stories published. Since then, his first novel,  *All Those Years Ago*, was published, *Summer Heat*, his fifth novel, was published in May 2012 and his bestseller, *The Mansfield Killings*, based on a true story, was published in October 2012. To date, Scott has published 16 novels.

The Mansfield Killings and *The Killing Road* will soon be made into major motion pictures.

Now, Scott spends nearly all his time writing his next novel.

Scott lives in Mansfield, Ohio, where most of his novels take place, with his wife, Deb.

Visit his web site, **www.scottcfields.com** to learn more.

www.ingramcontent.com/pod-product-compliance
Lightning Source LLC
Chambersburg PA
CBHW051241250626
47155CB00009B/3113